Redefining the Rules

Emily Tudor

For those who prefer dancing in the rain, rather than waiting for the storm to pass.

And for Lauren, just because.

Playlist

Afterglow - Ed Sheeran
All My Love - Noah Kahan
The Blue - Gracie Abrams
Boys Like You - Who is Fancy
Cinema - Harry Styles
Cool About It - Boygenius
Cut to the Feeling - Carly Rae Jepsen
Dancing With Our Hands Tied (Taylor's
Version) - Taylor Swift
Diana - One Direction
Disconnected - 5 Seconds of Summer
Fearless (Taylor's Version) - Taylor Swift
Francesca - Hozier
Get Him Back! - Olivia Rodrigo
Good Looking - Suki Waterhouse
How You Get the Girl (Taylor's Version) - Taylor Swift
In My Head - Ariana Grande
Movies - Conan Gray
Reckless Driving - Lizzy McAlpine
Say Yes To Heaven - Lana Del Ray
Send My Love (To Your New Lover) - Adele
State of Grace (Taylor's Version) - Taylor Swift
Sunshine Baby - The Japanese House
Supercut - Lorde
Vibes - Chase Atlantic
What Was Mine - Sarah Kinsley
2 / 14 - The Band CAMINO

"But I just want to say that all this nothing has meant more to me than so many somethings."
— Kathleen Kelly (You've Got Mail)

PROLOGUE

Jacks

October 1st, 2020

"You're wrong. The best rom-com of all time is *You've Got Mail*," I say to my teammate, roommate, and best friend as we lace up our skates before practice.

"No, *you're* wrong. My mom and I used to watch *How to Lose a Guy in 10 Days* all the time when I was growing up, and nothing comes close to it," Grant argues back.

"This is ridiculous. You're telling me that two booksellers who initially hate each other but spark an online romance unknowingly and have to reconcile their feelings isn't one of the best plots of a movie ever?" I pause before talking again. "Oh right, I forgot about your intense dislike of books. That *must* be why you hate the greatest rom-com of all time."

"I have nothing against books. You know I prefer movies because books make me sleepy. Also, not all of us grew up with two parents madly in love, or with your mom, who used to read you romance novels before bedtime." Grant Carter is the only guy who seems allergic to books and anything romance. My best friend has it easy with the ladies, since he's over six feet tall, has brown hair, and a charisma that makes most people melt.

Damn. I regret telling him about that. "I'm not ashamed. That little tidbit of information helps with girls anyway," I say as I stand up from the bench I was sitting on.

"Jacks, don't even make me say it." He pats my back as he walks past me. Yeah, maybe it helps me speak and understand women better than most, but that doesn't mean it has helped *me.* I've never had a girlfriend.

Like ever.

Sure, people have been interested in me before, and I've even been on a few dates since coming to college, but nothing has stuck. Nothing has *ever* stuck. I keep waiting for the butterflies and jittery feelings that are supposed to happen when you feel yourself falling, but I've never felt those. At this point, I don't know if I ever will.

I think at this point, I've accepted that the love my parents have is once in a lifetime, and I might not be destined for the same future. Even if I *want* that someday, it's not guaranteed.

Maybe I'm the problem? Nope. I'm not going there today. I have to focus, not fall down one of those spirals where I think I'm not good enough to have love. Plus, we have practice today, and I need to be on my game. Grant said that since the two senior defensemen are graduating at the end of this year, we have a chance to be starters next year as *sophomores.*

With a lot of hard work and practice, it could actually be true. Thankfully Grant and I work well on the ice. We tried out together, and ever since then we've been attached at the hip. We live together, play the same sport, and just fell into our friendship. He may annoy the shit out of me sometimes, but he's one of the greatest guys I know.

And at Grand Mountain, those can be hard to come by. We're a small liberal arts college and a big sports school. That means that a lot of jock assholes go to this school, but Grant's one of the good ones, and I like having him around.

I grab all my shit and head to the rink entrance from the locker room. As I step onto the ice, it all comes rushing at me. Grant told me once that he loves the escape that hockey provides him, along with the adrenaline.

I like hockey because it was the very first thing I fell in love with. My parents signed me up for junior hockey when I was six, and I was a natural. But nothing beats the feeling of scoring your first goal, and when I did, I knew I was in the right place—on the ice. Hockey has been a constant in my life since I was little, and no matter what, I know it'll always be there for me.

Coach starts talking like he usually does, and I don't really listen to what he's saying. I just want to start practicing. Practice always makes me feel all giddy, and I can't wait another second before he dismisses us to start doing drills.

Fifteen minutes later, Coach splits us all off into groups, and practice begins. Grant and I are with the defensemen and we're working on blue line shuffles. Grant and I are paired off as usual, and before we start the drill, I notice a weird look on his face.

"What?" I ask him.

"Nothing. I just think it's weird having all these cameras here," he says as he looks around the rink.

"What the hell are you talking about?" I ask him, and sure enough, when I peer around, a bunch of photographers are in the stands and behind the nets on both sides. *What's going on?*

"I *knew* you were zoned out while Coach was talking. He told us that since the team won our division last year, the school is doing a profile for the paper." Grant smacks my shoulder as he gets ready for the drill we're doing. He lines the pucks up on the blue line, and when he's done, he shoots me a puck that we can use. As we start passing it between us and doing the drill, I hear the snap of the cameras. Usually nothing bothers me while I'm on the ice, but someone's using flash, which isn't allowed. As I lift my head up to politely tell them to turn their flash off, my legs freeze and my skate catches on something on the ice, causing me to fall.

Fuck, that hurt. Grant skates over to me and offers me his hand to help me up. I take it and look back to where the flash came from. *Where did she go?* The person behind that camera was a girl I've never seen before, and one of the most beautiful people I've ever seen. Fuck, she was gorgeous. Maybe I can find her after practice is over.

An hour and a half later, I shuffle out of the locker room, hoping to find this mystery girl that has my stomach in knots. I sweep my gaze over the stands, and just when I think she left already, a flash of blonde hair catches my eye.

Fuck. What do I say to her? And why am I nervous right now? This girl has a bunch of cute freckles all over her face, blue eyes, and an aura that I find myself drawn too for some reason. I'm too busy in my thoughts to notice that she's heading my way. Fuck. What should I do? Do I introduce myself? Do I act casual? Fuck, this seems so much easier in the movies.

"Number 86, right?" she asks me, and I look around, thinking she's not talking to me. "The one who fell on the ice earlier?"

"Fuck. Yes, that was me. Sorry." I'm making a gigantic fool of myself right now. This is the worst thing to ever happen to me.

"I was in charge of photographing the defenseman for the article, but I got a few good pictures that I thought you might want. You know, for social media and stuff." She throws a smile at me, and my knees feel weak again.

Is this it? Is this the feeling?

"Yeah, sure. I always love a good action shot." *Why did I say that?*

"What's your name so I can email them to you?"

"Jacks. Jacks Moore. Two O's. My email is my first and last name, separated by an underscore." *Ask what her name is, asshole.* "And your name is…?"

"Claire Canes." She smiles at me as she closes the little notebook she was writing in. *God, that smile was perfect. How do I get her to do it again?*

"So tell me, Claire Canes, how long have you been photographing sports?"

"Since this semester, when the athletic director allowed it," she says to me when I notice a presence beside me.

"Jacks, who might this be?" Grant asks as he saddles up next to me. I *knew* he was going to do this. When I was rushing in the locker room, he kept asking me questions, but I ignored them all so I wouldn't miss this girl. Now he's going to ruin it.

She holds her hand out to him. "Claire Canes. I took a few photos of you guys practicing, and I figured you might want them."

"Oh, I hope you have a few pictures of this guy falling." Grant elbows me, and I smile, trying to hide the fact that I want to hit him back. "I'd love to have that to make fun of him with."

"I do, but out of respect, I'm declining to give you them," she chuckles and then takes her notebook back out. "I did take some good ones of you, Grant. I'll email those to you later."

"How'd you know my name?" he asks her, and I'd like to know the same thing.

"Everyone around school knows you, Carter. You're a golden retriever on skates." I can't say that it doesn't sting that she knows him and not me. Whatever. "Keep an eye out for my email, boys. I have to edit them first, but you should have them by the end of the week."

"Thanks, Claire. Appreciate it!" Grant waves to her as she leaves, and I'm stuck standing here looking like an idiot. Grant turns to face me before I grab my bag and split. "Are we going to talk about it?"

"About what?" I coyly say to him.

"You busting your ass on the ice when you first looked at her. I've never seen you look so starstruck before. I'm not sure if I should be concerned or excited."

"You should be nothing."

"Yeah, right. I can see it in your eyes. You like that girl." He smiles at that.

"She's pretty, yes. And from my short conversation with her, I wouldn't be opposed to speaking to her again."

"Maybe you can email back and forth and fall in love that way. That sounds like a rom-com screenplay waiting to happen," Grant jokes with me. Dammit. He's never going to let me hear the end of this, and I might be too much of a wuss to do anything about it.

"G, that is literally *You've Got Mail!*" I yell at him as we exit the rink. I don't know if anything will happen with Claire and me, but damn, I hope something does. I've surely never just *looked* at someone and had the feeling I did.

Maybe it's fate, or destiny, that I saw her here today. But as Annie Reed once said, "Destiny is something we've invented because we can't stand the fact that everything that happens is accidental."

1

Claire

January 7th, 2022

"You're breaking up with me on our anniversary? Are you fucking serious, Clay?" I'm seething right now. *Seething.* I planned a whole night to celebrate, and when he texted me earlier about wanting to talk tonight, I never would've assumed *this* was what he wanted to talk about.

"We're headed in different directions, Claire Bear."

God, I *hate* when he calls me that. You'd think after dating for three years he would know that, but what did I expect? He forgot I had a peanut allergy once and almost killed me when he made me a sandwich one day. That should've been a huge red flag, but there I go again, always looking for the best in people who don't deserve it.

There's nobody to blame but myself.

"Different directions? What happened to the life we had planned for? I thought that was what *you* wanted? Are you just throwing that out the window?" Clay and I have been dating since our senior year in high school. He was a baseball player, and I was the girl taking pictures of sports games for the yearbook. I got hit by a foul ball one day, and Clay came to my rescue. He brought me an ice pack, and we sat and talked. It was sweet, but now I wish *he* was the one who would get hit by a foul ball.

"We're in over our heads. We're still young, Claire. We have our whole lives ahead of us, and I don't want to waste it being tied down—"

"*Tied down?* Is this a joke? You were the one who laid our entire lives out when I agreed to follow you here for college!" Granted, Grand Mountain has a wonderful photography program, but it wasn't high on my list when I was trying to choose a college. Clay was the one who convinced me to come here with him, saying that we'd have the time of our lives growing together in a new place.

What a fucking lie *that* was. And here I am, the girl dumb enough to believe it.

"Claire Bear, I'm sorry...I just..." He glances at the floor as if he can't look me in the eyes as he breaks up with me.

"Please stop calling me that," I seethe at him. "Are you doing this because you're not in love with me anymore or because you want to start acting like your douchebag single friends?" Most of his friends aren't the relationship type. I'd cringe at how they'd talk about women whenever I was around them. I remember being glad that Clay wasn't like them, but now I think maybe he is, or maybe he wants to be.

"This isn't about my friends, Claire. I couldn't keep this from you anymore. I don't love you anymore. I'm sorry. I don't think this relationship is doing anything for either of us anymore."

Was my love not enough to keep this relationship going? Was what I put into this relationship not enough? God, I'm such an idiot. "So, all the shit we talked about concerning our future was what? A fantasy? You were talking about our wedding a couple of days ago, and now you're breaking up with me? It doesn't make any fucking sense, Clay."

"Claire, you need to calm down."

Oh, absolutely not. "Clay, I've been nothing but a dutiful girlfriend to you for three years, and all I got back was false promises! Excuse me for reacting appropriately for the first time in my life!" I'm not one to yell. I'm a naturally quiet person, but I can't do that in this situation. I'm pissed off.

"Look, I'm gonna go. I'm really sorry it had to happen this way, but I'll never forget how good of a girlfriend you were. I hope we can get back to being friends someday."

"So, I'm not good enough to love as your girlfriend, but I'm good enough to have as a friend after you've broken my heart?" No way. I gave my entire life to Clay. I followed him to Virginia from our small hometown in Delaware just so he could live out his dream of playing baseball for this school, and he repays me by breaking up with me on our anniversary of all days. I'm done being a pushover, and I'm done being nice to people who don't deserve my kindness.

"Goodbye, Claire," he says as he walks out of my dorm.

"Bye, Clay," I softly say as he gets out of my earshot. I didn't expect tonight to go how it did, but as I wait for myself to cry about my failed three-year relationship, nothing comes. I think part of me is relieved over this, but I also feel...cheated in a way. It seems like Clay had some sort of ulterior motive for doing what he did tonight. Sure, he was distant the past few weeks, but I thought he was just tired from his pre-season training.

Stupid me for being so naive that I missed all the signs.

God, I'm so sick of myself. All I ever do is look for

the best in people and get hurt in the process. I've given people in my life more chances than they deserve, and the only thing I get in return is being stuck in a never-ending cycle of hurt.

I whip out my phone before I start my own personal pity party and text my roommate, who I kicked out of our room tonight to make this happen.

Claire: How fast can you get to our dorm with ice cream?
Sara: What the fuck did he do?
Sara: Don't tell me now.
Sara: Give me fifteen minutes, and I'll be there.
Claire: I love you, thank you.
Sara: I love you too.

When I put my phone down, the realization of tonight hits me in the chest, and I cave in on myself. How could I have been so stupid? I've been on edge for the past few weeks, and instead of talking to Clay about the distance I felt between us, I let it sit. *Did I want this to happen? Did I want him to do this to us?* We haven't been the same since last semester, and I never knew why. I think deep down I knew where we were headed, but part of me latched onto the familiarity of Clay and I. Now that it's over, I'm not breaking down like I should be.

Breakups suck, but there's still a weird feeling in my gut. Is it sadness? Longing for the future I could've had? Relief that a relationship that no longer suited me is over? Guilt? I honestly don't know. But I don't trust Clay. I don't know if I ever did, deep down.

I'm on my floor for who knows how long when I hear my door open with a bang. "Where is that stupid son of a bitch, and can I finally tell you how much I hated him?" Sara asks as she sweeps into the room.

"Gone."

She puts her bag on the floor before coming over to where I am. "Do you want to talk about it, or do you want to eat ice cream and watch a Christmas movie while I talk shit about him?"

Her question makes me smile, but I'm not sure I'm fully ready to unpack this all tonight. It's still too fresh. "Option B, please. Even though it's January, I'll watch Christmas movies anytime."

"Perfect," Sara says as she grabs two bowls to put the ice cream in. I've never been more thankful for someone right now. She didn't even hesitate to come running when I called her. Our relationship has grown exponentially over the past two years, but I never could've imagined someone like her in my life. Sure, I have some friends at home, but we all went our separate ways. We only keep in touch when we go home for breaks because of how busy we are, which is fine. But Sara is a once in a lifetime friend. Even if I came to Grand Mountain for Clay, I'll always be thankful that this school brought Sara and me together. She's a forever friend. That, I am certain of.

But maybe forever has always been a lie.

I guess I'll find out. Clay certainly didn't believe in that word, so why should I?

2

Jacks

January 2022

"How do I have an F already?" my best friend scoffs from across our dorm. We're a week into Spring semester, and I'm having a pretty good time. "What the fuck?"

Grant is not. "What's going on, G?"

"Collins gave us a quiz already, and I failed it. I'm fucking pissed."

"Obviously, I can see that." I throw a smile in his direction while he flips me off.

"Jacks, we have practice tonight. Coach gets notified when our grades slip, you know that." Grant sighs as he slips his hand down his face, clearly stressed about this.

"G, it's going to be fine. It's just one grade. You know a lot of professors don't update their grades regularly. Maybe talk to Collins after class or something. Let him know your dilemma."

"Dude, I can't do that. I'll just figure something out on my own."

"Grant, you know it's not bad to ask for help." I raise my eyebrows at him and he quickly changes the subject like he always does.

"Who assigns summer reading anymore, anyway? I haven't had to do that since middle school, and even then, I still forged my mom's signature." He sighs heavily before continuing. "It's just ridiculous."

"Yes, you've mentioned that." When I say that, he slides down his chair and onto our floor. Always one for dramatics. I grab my AirPods and slide them back into my ears as Grant continues ranting. I find that it's best to just let him get it all out in one go and then give my advice—if he wants it. I'm halfway through an Ed Sheeran song when Brendan practically kicks our door open. I knew he was coming over because he texted our group chat earlier, but I didn't think he'd get here so fast.

"Woah, G. Are you good? I don't think I've ever heard you talk that fast…" Brendan asks him.

"I'm fine, just failing a class one week into the semester, and now I'm never going to succeed in life."

"Wow, and I thought my little sister was dramatic when she cries over fictional characters in books." Brendan looks at me. "Grant might be giving her a run for her money."

"Your sister is 100 percent valid in any reaction she has while reading, Brendan. Grant's just jumping to the worst-case scenario and not considering that it's the *first week* of the semester," I tell him while Grant keeps sulking. "Is your week going as bad as his?"

Brendan throws a smirk my way. "No. It's been fine. Not good or bad, just fine."

"Great, so the only one loving life right now is Jacks. The rest of us are screwed if this is how the semester is starting," Grant groans. He's one of my best friends, but there's nobody on the planet more dramatic than him. I know he's afraid of failing and everything, but someone besides me needs to tell this guy that he's worth more than his grades.

"So, Jacks…" Brendan trails off. *Fuck, I knew this was going to happen.*

"Just fucking say it, Brendan." I look over at Grant and he seems happy to have the conversation switch off him and onto me.

"Grant told me that you had class with Claire last night. How was that? Did you finally get the courage to say anything or did you chicken out like usual?"

Yeah, so I have a class with a girl I've had a crush on for a while. Basically, ever since I laid eyes on her. I really regret telling Grant that I saw her in class last night. I should've known it was going to turn into a whole thing like it usually does. Not only does Grant make fun of me about it twenty-four seven, but now they've banded together to piss me off.

"First of all, I don't chicken out—she has a boyfriend. It's called being respectful!" I deflect and they both know it.

"Jacks, you have *two* classes with her this semester. Your genetics lecture three times a week, and interpersonal communication on Thursday nights. I think the universe is sending you a sign or some shit. It's fate." Grant smiles at me.

"You saying the word fate is going to send me into a coma. Guys, she's taken, so drop it," I tell them while I go to put my AirPods back on. I want to leave this conversation. I want to shrink into the walls and disappear. It's bad enough that I've never been in love or a serious long-term relationship, but them constantly reminding me about it doesn't help either.

"Just because there's a goalie doesn't mean you can't score..." Brendan smiles when he says that.

"Seriously dude?" Grant shakes his head at him.

"Eww, Brendan. Never say that again," I tell him.

"What? It's true!" He throws his hands up in

protest.

I throw one of my pillows at him. "Don't be gross."

The three of us are silent for a few seconds before Grant says something that makes my breath hitch. "If she's taken, how come I saw her boyfriend all over some girl from the dance team?"

Did they break up? If they did, it's not like it would make a difference...right? I still don't know how to talk to someone that I have weird feelings for. How do you approach a girl you like without looking like a complete idiot?

"Ooo...the plot thickens!" Brendan says.

"Can we just drop this and study like we were supposed to? Grant and I have practice in a few hours and the team is going to want to go out after. I need to get *something* done before then," I ask, and the two of them share a knowing look before nodding.

"Are we going to the library or staying here?" Brendan asks, probably already knowing that answer.

"I'm not stepping foot into the library unless I have to. Let's chill in the lounge. That way Jacks can play us one of his movie soundtracks that he loves so much." Grant slaps me on the shoulder and I look over at him.

"You complain about it now, but when you start humming to *Dreams* by The Cranberries, I don't want to hear it."

"Yeah, whatever. Let's just hope your speaker doesn't end up in the shower at some point," Grant says while Brendan throws his arms around our shoulders.

"Now children...let's not fight."

3

Claire

I feel something knock against my face as I zone out while in the dining hall. When I look down, I notice a strawberry in my lap. How did that get there?

"Claire!" someone shouts in front of me and I'm knocked out of my daydream or whatever I was doing. When I look up, Sara and Jess are sitting across from me, their faces concerned.

"What was that for?" I ask them, utterly confused.

"We've been asking you questions for five minutes and you haven't answered a single one of them," Jess tells me. "Are you doing okay? I know it's been a rough start to the semester for you."

Yeah...rough. My long time boyfriend broke up with me and now I spend every day looking back on the whole relationship and wondering what I did wrong. The only thing I've found is that I captured a beautiful picture of what we had in my mind, only to find in the end that it wasn't even gallery worthy. Every scenario I think of comes back to bite me in the ass. Looking back now, all the good parts of our relationship were in my head. I filled in the gaps of what *I* wanted us to be like, but turns out he never had the same vision that I did.

But yeah, I'm totally fine. Mostly I feel duped, sad, angry, and pissed.

I let him drag me along for so long, feeling unfulfilled but trying my best to keep us afloat, when he was giving me empty promises that would eventually lead to my broken heart.

Did I mention I was pissed?

"Yeah, I'm fine," I say as to not worry them.

"Claire, be for real right now...are you?" Sara asks me.

"Yes. I'm alright."

"Then why haven't you talked to us about it yet? I've been waiting to tell you all the things I hated about him while you guys were dating. I even made a whole PowerPoint about it. It's very cohesive." That's Jess for you in a nutshell.

Sara and I met her on the first day of freshman orientation. The three of us stuck together like a bunch of lost puppies, and we've been friends ever since. Jess has strawberry blonde hair, a bunch of freckles, and the prettiest hazel eyes I've ever seen. She's around the same height as me—5'6"—and her laugh is one of my favorite things about her. Sara, on the other hand, has long jet-black hair and is a few inches taller than Jess and me. Her brown eyes are almost as dark as her hair. We are complete opposites. She dresses in dark or earth-toned colors, and I usually prefer pastels. She always jokes that she's the black cat in our friendship, and I'd agree with that assessment.

"Guys, I swear I'm okay. I'm getting through it and trying to move on, explaining why I haven't talked about it yet. I'm trying this new thing where I don't care. It's quite helpful." I smile to further show them just how alright I am, but based on their faces, they aren't buying my bullshit.

"Claire, this isn't healthy. It's okay to be upset, but you *have* to talk about what you're feeling, or else it'll eat you alive." Fuck. Jess is definitely right, but where would I even begin? Most of this is all my fault.

"She's right, Claire. I don't want you to shove your feelings down like you always do. It's time for you to get pissed and tell us how small his dick is or something," Sara tells me.

"I *am* pissed. I just don't want to be—"

"Mean? Babes, he was the one to break your heart. You no longer have to protect your true feelings for fear of coming across as mean because he's not here anymore. So, it doesn't matter. If you're pissed, then let me come over tonight and present my PowerPoint. We can get drunk and angry in the comfort of your dorm where nobody but us can hear you call him whatever names you want to." Jess puts her hand over where mine rests on the table and I sigh heavily at them.

"Fine. I guess it's time. It's not like I want him to come crawling back and apologize, right?" Am I convincing them or myself? I don't think that would be best, though. Our relationship was too...comfortable. It was too easy in the moment, but now that I'm away from it, I realize that I wasn't actually happy. I was just agreeable.

I never want to be like that again. I want to fall in love in the future and feel the butterflies and giddiness that comes with finding the right person, the person that fits with you, but also challenges you. I thought I had that with Clay. Maybe I did in the start, but soon those butterflies in my stomach died. All that was left was me chasing the feeling I *once* had that didn't stay.

On second thought, Clay crawling back to me while I get to break his heart when I say no doesn't sound so bad...

No. No. I shove that thought down because that is *not* who I am. I'm not petty like that. *But maybe sometimes I need to be...*

"Exactly. That's the spirit, girl! I'll grab some wine before I come over later, but make sure you have ice cream that we can eat too." Jess smiles at me.

"We're plenty stocked up. I bought like six cartons the day that motherfucker did what he did..." Sara trails off as she thinks back to when we watched movies all night and ate ice cream. It was the best. "I can't wait until you find someone a thousand times hotter than him, and who treats you how you deserve. That will be the ultimate 'fuck you' to Clay."

"Woah, Sar. I don't think I'm in the moving on stage quite yet," I tell her.

"Yeah, way to jump like four steps, girl." Jess smiles at her as Sara rolls her eyes.

I take a beat before I speak again, "Thank you, guys. For all the support and everything you've done to help me the past few weeks. I promise I'll stop pretending like I'm fine, okay?"

"No need to thank us," Jess says as she looks at Sara.

"You would do the same for us, babe," Sara tells me.

"You guys are the best. I truly don't know what I'd —" I stop what I'm saying because I notice that neither of them is looking at me anymore, they're looking *through* me, at whatever is behind me. When I turn, I see part of the hockey team entering the dining hall. There's only one on our campus because Grand Mountain is small, so you're bound to see the whole school here at some point. The good thing is that the food is decent. The bad thing is that if you're trying to avoid someone, you can't. The campus is too small for that to be possible. Luckily, I haven't seen Clay at all. I'm afraid I'd take one look at him and punch him, which wouldn't be the worst thing in the world.

Lucky for me, I know most of the athletes at this school. Since I photograph all the sports games here at Grand Mountain, I've become familiar with most of the players. They all treat me pretty well, and I'm *very* passionate about photography. What once was a hobby on weekends is now what I hope to do with the rest of my life. I'm glad the athletic director let me work with the department so I could get some experience for the future. I started photographing the teams last year, and I *love* doing it. It's just like it was in high school, only way more exciting. High school sports are great, but there's something about college sports that is much more riveting.

I lock eyes with one of the hockey players and a good friend of mine, Justin. He waves at me and comes over to where I sit.

"What's up, Canes? How's this semester treating you so far?" he asks me while looking at Jess and Sara, shooting them a wave before he leans down to hug me.

I laugh at him before answering. "It's been interesting for sure. How about you? How's the team looking?" I ask as I sweep over the remaining players. Some of them have separated from the group to talk to other people they know, and a few others have sat down at a huge table. I recognize some of them, they're mostly sophomores, and I assume the others are new freshmen on the team. I haven't become too familiar with them yet, but when the games pick back up in a few weeks, I'm sure that'll change.

"It's been alright. You know how it is. Coach is still

making the freshman and sophomores eat lunch together on practice days. It's a wonderfully awkward tradition, but it's tradition nonetheless," Justin tells me. He's a good-looking guy. He's around 5'11", with brown hair that he usually pulls into a man bun. He's got a typical athletic build, and he plays left wing for Grand Mountain. He's pretty good, and I love watching him play.

"I'm glad. How's that boyfriend of yours?" I ask him.

"Cute as hell even though he gets on my nerves sometimes." He smiles. Justin has been dating his boyfriend Miles for almost a year. Miles and I often sit with each other at their games when I'm not photographing the team. He's a wonderful person to watch hockey with, even though he never knows what's going on, but he tries his best.

"I can't wait until your games start up again so I can reteach him everything he probably forgot over mid-semester break."

"Does that mean you're game this semester for team pictures?" I nod. "Fuck yes. That's what's up!" He high fives me, and I see another player approaching Justin from behind.

"Candy Canes! What's up girl?" Grant Carter asks me, and I feign a laugh at that *stupid* nickname he gave me last semester. I emailed him a few shots from a practice I photographed and he responded with that nickname and a thumbs-up emoji. He's a pretty funny guy. I don't know him that well—I only know *of* him—but he's universally adored on campus, and he's not a douche, so that's a win I'd say. He's got a nice face too, but he's not my type. I'm not even sure *what* my type is anymore. Maybe I don't have one? I have no clue.

"Not much, Carter. How's the semester?" I ask and his face falls. *Oh shit.* It's only been two weeks. How bad could he be doing already? *At least someone else is having a shitty semester so early in.*

"It could be better, but it can only go up from here." He smiles. "Hopefully."

The three of us talk for a few more minutes before Justin excuses himself to go meet Miles at their table. Another player comes up next to Grant and starts to say something quietly to him, but Grant cuts him off with a huge smile on his face.

"Jacks, you *must* remember Claire. She was the one who photographed you falling on your face at practice last year. Thanks for emailing me that by the way," Grant winks at me and I awkwardly laugh. When I look over at Jacks, he looks *super* uncomfortable, like he can't speak. I remember taking that picture and talking to these two after practice. It was nice. I think we might be in some of the same classes this semester, including the genetics lecture I decided to take as an elective. It has nothing to do with my major—photography with a minor in communication—but I've always found biology to be easy, so it's a win-win.

Jacks is cute, but in a shy way. He's got sandy blond hair, is slightly taller than Grant, and is skinny but muscular. His eyes are hazel, and his hair falls just the right way. I've seen him play, and if you told me that was the same person that I saw on the ice standing in front of me right now, I would think you're lying.

"Yeah, hi. Nice to see you again," he says, avoiding eye contact.

"Sorry for sending Grant that photo, I'm sure he probably made it a meme or something." I awkwardly laugh.

"Grant made an animated GIF, actually. It was my fault for falling, your phenomenal photography skills were just lucky to capture it." Jacks tells me.

Phenomenal? "Well, thanks. Grant any chance you could send me that GIF? I'd love to see it." When I look over at him, he's smiling from ear to ear.

"Oh, of course. I'll email it to you." A few seconds of silence pass before Jacks breaks the tension.

"Grant, we should probably..." He trails off, motioning toward their table.

"Oh, right. Well, it was nice to see you again, Claire. I'm sure we'll be seeing you at some games soon."

"You bet. Good to see you guys." I throw a small wave at them as they leave, and when I turn back to my friends, they look starstruck. "What?"

"I didn't know you were that close with Grant motherfucking Carter! Why haven't you mentioned this before?"

"Jess, we aren't that close. That was *maybe* the third time I've talked to him in person, and why does your face look like that?"

"He's hot. Like, given the chance I would climb him hot." Jess fans herself as she says that.

"Gross," Sara says.

"Jess, I'm not setting you up, so don't even ask me. I barely know him, and unlike most jocks at this school, he's an actual good guy. He doesn't seem like the type to go for a one-night stand. Don't make me pour a glass of cold water on you in the middle of the dining hall," I threaten and she waves a napkin like a white flag.

"Fine. But can I at least come watch the games with you this semester? I'm not able to touch, but a girl can still look..." Sara rolls her eyes at Jess again, and I laugh as the three of us continue to eat lunch together before class.

I might've lost someone I thought I was going to love forever, but these two have shown me that sometimes it's not about what you've been through. It's about how you move on and continue to laugh despite it all that defines you the most. I might feel like I'm waiting to fall apart right now, but I know these two will carefully patch the pieces back up when I need them to, and I'll let them.

4

Jacks

"Did you get my email?" I ask the girl who sits a few seats away from me in my genetics lecture.

Hadleigh Baker. Grant's possible tutor for Intro to Lit this semester if he makes a good impression, and she agrees. Grant can come on strong when he's desperate, so it could go either way after this class.

She turns her head to look at me. Class hasn't started yet, so we have some time. "I did. Will he be waiting after class? I have some time before my next one."

"He should be. I told him what building and room number we're in," I tell her as I take out my computer. Hadleigh's super smart. I've had a few general classes with her, and she always participates and gets all the answers right. I like to think I'm generally pretty smart, but she's on Einstein's level of genius.

She looks like she's about to say something else, but opts not to. I press her anyway, wondering what could make her nervous to ask me. "Are you okay?"

"What's he like? Is he an asshole?"

"*I* don't think he's an asshole. He's nice, but he can be a bit dramatic sometimes. You're going to love him." I smile at her and she rolls her eyes.

"Okay, well that's good."

"It's going to be great." I realize in this moment that I never told Grant her name, or what she looks like. Shit. Is this going to be weird? No, I think it'll be fine.

Right?

Well, it's not my problem. I'm passing with flying colors. Grant can figure it out, he'll be okay.

As I pull my notes up on my computer, I see a flash of blonde hair out of the corner of my eye. I don't even have to look because I already know who it is. *God, she gets prettier every time I see her.* It's not fucking fair. Nobody should be *that* beautiful. And I shouldn't be so afraid of going up and speaking to her, but I am.

Life just isn't fair.

When I saw her in the dining hall the other day, I thought I was having a heart attack. It turns out that I can barely look at her without feeling like I got the wind knocked out of me. That's how I know that I'm fucked. Maybe by senior year, I'll have the courage to say something to her, to become friends maybe. I don't know why I'm so bad at this. I've never had an issue talking to anyone before, but with her it's different.

Very different, and I don't know why.

Maybe today will be the day I finally say something. Maybe I can pretend I'm struggling with the homework and can ask her to check it for me. That's easy enough, right? One classmate asking another classmate for help on these stupid worksheets that we have to do.

She sits down in her usual spot a few rows in front of me, and I know I'm going to spend another entire class fantasizing about having the courage to say something to her.

After class ends, I look around for Hadleigh so I can properly introduce her to Grant, but I don't find her. *Shit.* Where could she have gone? I grab my bookbag and head for the door, only to peak out and find that she's already talking to Grant. Oh good, they're getting acquainted. Grant's wearing hockey apparel and has a weird look on his face. Okay…so maybe the conversation isn't going so well after all. I had a feeling he would fuck this up. He can come on strong, especially when he needs help, and some people who don't know him won't know that. When Grant cares about you, you'll know.

I notice his body turn, and it looks like he's trying to get away. I walk toward the two of them. "Grant, this is the girl I was telling you about, the one who can help you pass Intro to Lit this semester." Why does his face look like that? And what is up with the air around these two? I feel like I just walked straight into a volcano as I came over here.

Grant holds out his hands a few seconds later, clearly trying to save whatever happened before I came over here. "I'm Grant, and I would very much appreciate your help. That is if you're available and willing to tutor this *hockey boy*."

What the fuck does that mean? Why did he just wink at her like that? I'm so damn confused. She doesn't say a word, and I don't know Hadleigh that well, but I've never seen her look how she does right now. I don't even know if pissed describes it. What the fuck did he say to her before I got over here? She stands where she is, just staring at his hand that's held out. I almost think she's going to just walk away, but she surprises me with what she ends up saying.

"Hadleigh." After that, she turns and walks away. Grant stands stagnant for a minute before he's knocked out of his haze and starts to follow after her, leaving me here by myself.

Well, that could've gone better, but maybe it'll be fine.

I sure hope she can tutor him because the team can't lose Grant off defense. We work well together, and it'd be a pain in the ass to have to work with one of the new freshmen that aren't used to college hockey yet.

"Jacks?" I hear someone say, and when I turn around, I feel my breath hitch in my throat. *Jesus, when is that going to stop?*

"Hey, Claire. What's up?"

"Was that Grant? He's not in our class, is he?"

"No, he's not." I run a hand through my hair, suddenly feeling really nervous. "Hadleigh might tutor him this semester for a class he's failing, and I told him to meet me after so I could introduce them."

"Grant's failing something already? I meant to ask him about it the other day when I saw you guys in the dining hall. He looked a bit...stressed. I could tell something was weighing on him." This must be a sick joke. Not only is she beautiful, but she's nice as fuck too.

Claire has long blonde hair, a thousand freckles, and blue eyes that match the sky. She's around 5'6", I think, and has the prettiest smile that I've ever seen.

But she's not single, so there's nothing I can do. Not like I would, but a guy can dream, right? "Yeah, that would be what. He'll be fine though. Hadleigh's a genius. I just hope he didn't kill his chances with whatever first impression he laid on her."

She smiles when I say that. *I made her smile.* Fuck, I feel like I just won the lottery. Why did that feel so good? "As far as first impressions go, I don't think anyone could beat ours."

"Ah, yes. Me falling on my face probably left a

lasting impression on you. I'm sure you've told all your friends about the hockey player who can barely skate."

"Oh no, of course not." An awkward silence comes over the two of us, and I silently berate myself in my head for saying something so stupid. "I may have posted it on my Instagram for the entire school to see, but other than that nobody knows."

At that we both laugh, and I realize this is the first time I'm hearing that come out of her mouth. God, her boyfriend is so lucky. If I was him, I'd try to make her laugh all the time, just so I could hear that sound. Okay so, she's beautiful, nice, and funny? Every time I learn more about her, I want to know more. But I can't. I can't do anything knowing she's in a relationship, regardless of whatever Grant and Brendan said the other day.

It's not like I want her to be my girlfriend. I just want to know more about her every time I talk to her. Whenever we have these short conversations, I find myself yearning for more, and that's never happened to me before. She just has this way of captivating me, and I'm not sure why.

"Well thanks for that. That must explain why my follow count has gone up. People must feel bad for me knowing that I play hockey and can't concentrate with a camera on me."

She chuckles again. "No problem. I also sent a few pictures to ESPN, but they have yet to respond."

"Well if they reach out asking me for a comment, I'll be sure to mention you as the talented photographer who captured my essence perfectly." *Stop flirting, asshole. She has a boyfriend.*

"Talented, huh?" I notice her flushed cheeks and hope that I didn't make her uncomfortable.

"Absolutely. I've seen your work all over the website for athletics. It's insane what you can do behind a camera." I truly mean that. I have no idea how to work those fancy ass cameras I see people using, but it's impressive.

"Well thanks. I'll try to get some better ones of you when your games start up again," she smiles at me, just as her phone buzzes. "I have another class soon, but I'll see you Wednesday?"

"Not if I see you there first!" *Fucking hell. Why did I say that?*

With that, she giggles and walks away.

God, I'm such an idiot. I think about texting Grant to see where he ended up, but I decide not to. I'll see him later and he can fill me in. For now, I navigate to my next class, with a smile pasted on my face after the short conversation I had with a girl that barely knows I exist.

5

Claire

"HE WHAT?" I yell as I slam my door closed behind me. I'm fuming. No, I've gone right past fuming and straight to murderous.

"Woah, girl. Take a few breaths. You look like you're ready to make a trap and shove Clay into it like in *Saw*," Sara tells me, as she comes over to where I'm burning a hole into the floor.

"Maybe I am. Please elaborate on the text you sent me," I seethe at her as I throw my bag to the side and head for the freezer we have in our dorm. If what she tells me is true, then I'm going to need ice cream. Lots of it. Thankfully, it's Friday, so if she's right, then I can spend the weekend sulking.

"He has a new girlfriend."

"Okay, but how do you know?" I'm double-checking with her because I don't believe that Clay would move on this fast.

Or it means that he was talking to this new girl on the side while we were still together. And if that's true, I don't know if I'll ever believe in my judgment ever again.

How could I have been so stupid?

Sara shows me her laptop—with a thousand Instagram tabs open—and she walks me through how she got to this conclusion. "Jess saw him walking to class with some girl. Apparently, he was holding her hand, and before they went their separate ways, they shared a *very* passionate kiss. Jess said she almost threw up on the spot when she saw it. The girl had a Grand Mountain logo on a bag she was carrying, so I looked at all the female athletic teams and sent pictures to Jess as I searched. Based on the description Jess gave me—tall, blonde, and skinny—I narrowed it down."

"Has she confirmed yet?" My entire body is cold. I can't tell if it's because of how pissed off I am, or how betrayed I feel. It's been two weeks since Clay broke my heart on our anniversary, and he's already moved onto someone else?

"She's on her way here right now with snacks and wine."

"Perfect." I grab the strawberry ice cream I took out of the freezer and stab my fork into it.

Sara rolls her eyes at me from the couch. "I know this sucks, but can you *please* just use a spoon for once? It's weird as fuck the way you eat ice cream."

I shake my head at her and I continue what I'm doing. I've always eaten in this way, ever since I can remember. My mom and dad always do it this way too, and I think it's just a quirk I picked up from them as a kid. *I miss them.* I should call them soon and update them on life and stuff, but I can't bring myself to pick up the phone.

They were the ones who told me that picking a college based on Clay would bite me in the ass, and I don't think I could handle telling them they were ultimately right. They never really liked him, and I thought by following Clay, I could prove to them that I was right in my decision.

I was okay at the start, but now I find myself regretting every move I've made since meeting Clay on the sidelines of the baseball field. Part of me wishes that I could travel back in time and warn my younger self about what would eventually happen, but I can't do that now. What's happened has happened, and there's nothing I can do to change that. Now he's moving on, and I'm stuck here wondering why I wasted the past three years with someone who could do what he did to me.

I'm not one hundred percent sure that he cheated on me, but it's looking that way. Normally, I would just try to let go and move on. But unfortunately for Clay, I'm not feeling like a pushover anymore.

I feel like messing with his head a little, just like he's doing to me. Where the fuck does he get off doing this practically in front of me? He had to know I'd find out sooner or later, being that he's flaunting this girl around in public.

Just as I'm lost in my thoughts, Jess storms in and heads right toward Sara. She doesn't say a word to either of us as she looks at her computer screen. A few seconds later, she points her finger at someone on the screen. I rush over to where they are and notice that the finger she's pointing with is her middle one. I stifle a laugh and look at the girl she's pointing at.

She's pretty, but she looks eerily similar to me. We have the same build, almost the same height, and the same color hair. It's creepy if I'm being honest. She's on the dance team for Grand Mountain.

It's also not her fault that she's in this mess. I'm always sick of people blaming the other person when they get cheated on. It's very obviously the fault of the whoever decided to cheat. Clay was the dumbass who made the decision, not her. I doubt Clay told her that we were together. He probably told her that we were broken up or on the verge of it.

Or he broke up with me as a promise to her. Anger has entered the chat again. God, I don't know what to believe right now.

"I hate that she's pretty," Sara says.

"I hate that when I saw her in person, she complimented my shoes," Jess tells us.

"I hate that her name is so pretty," I tell them.

Evangeline Hopkins. She sounds like the main character of a romance novel, and she has the looks to back that up. Fuck.

"I hate this entire situation so much. Did the past three years mean nothing to him? Why was I not good enough, but she is?" I look at my two best friends and I feel some tears start to brew. God, this sucks. I always knew in the back of my mind that this was a possibility. It always lingered that I was never going to live up to Clay's standards. I just never imagined that it would turn out to be true. He was always the one who brought up our future and talked about it. I thought him saying all this stuff about it meant that he wanted it with me, but maybe it was only *his* future. Not mine. Maybe I was the only one who saw both of us in those dreams, but he only saw himself.

I grab my ice cream off my desk, as I feel Jess rub circles on my back, telling me that she's here with me.

"So, how are we going to make this bastard pay? Personally, my favorite idea that has been brewing in my head the past few days is going full Carrie Underwood on his car. I'm talking carving your name on his seats, slashing his tires, and slamming his headlights in with one of those beautiful baseball bats he loves so much."

Sara and I look at each other and laugh. Jess is the

wild one of our little trio, and I'm grateful for her at this moment for making me laugh. "Jess, girl, no. I need to forget about all this and move on."

"Move on…like to someone else, so he gets jealous and comes crawling back? Or move on like finding a random hookup because that's doable. We can just go to the Hidden Bear or something," Jess smiles at us. "You're in need of a night out soon."

"Soon, yes. But not tonight. I just need to relax before I do something stupid." I don't make the best decisions when I'm drunk, so staying in should be all that's on the docket tonight.

"Okay, well what would you say to a PowerPoint presentation then?" Jess asks us.

"Here we go again." Sara rolls her eyes and abruptly shuts her laptop.

Jess reaches into her bag and pulls out three bottles of wine, along with her computer and an HDMI cord that she's plugging into our TV.

"Well, a *little* wine can't hurt, right?" I ask them, and we all laugh, ready to spend the night in and hopefully talk about how shitty Clay is.

So, it turns out wine *can* hurt. The three of us drank a bottle each, and now we're up to no good. Thankfully it's Saturday tomorrow because I can already feel a hangover coming.

By no good, I mean that we've hatched a plan to make Clay jealous and stick it back to him. I'm 90 percent sure that they're joking, but the wine has gone to my head and I'm seriously considering making this plan a reality.

"Okay, but who could she fake date? It would have

to be someone that would really get on his nerves or this plan won't work..." Sara trails off as she tries to drink more wine, but realizes her bottle is empty.

"Claire, you mentioned once that he hates hockey players, so why not ask Justin?" Jess asks me.

"He does hate hockey players..." Clay told me once that they're practically glorified figure skaters, and that he could play hockey in his sleep. I refrained from saying that he can't even skate because we were surrounded by all his friends, and I didn't want to come across as mean.

"Jess, he has a boyfriend. Everyone on campus knows that," Sara tells her. "What about that one kid... Ryan something or other. He has a decent face."

"That's a no go. My friend went on one date with him and he tried to fuck her after fifteen minutes. Really pushy, too. Stay away from him with a five-foot pole," Jess tells us, and I nod in agreement. I knew that already. Photographing the teams gives you a lot of insight into who the players really are. You see and hear a lot of shit at practice that can tell you a lot about someone's character, and Ryan has always rubbed me the wrong way. I can't tell if it's his demeanor or what, but he just strikes me as an asshole with fake charm.

As Sara and Jess keep talking, my drunken mind flashes to sandy blond hair, and hazel eyes that can never look at me fully. To a guy who left a very distinct impression on me when I hadn't even said a word to him.

And he called you talented, which was more praise than Clay said to you in three years.

Jacks would be perfect for this, and he seems nice enough. He's more introverted than I am, so it might take some convincing for him to do this with me.

I could ask him after their practice next Wednesday.

I'm sure their coach will let me photograph it, since they have their first game soon. The worst Jacks can do is say no, and maybe he could even point me to someone who could do it with me.

This is perfect. This is a good plan.

I'm done being nice. It's time for me to give Clay a taste of his own medicine. I'm going to make him jealous, and I'm going to do it with a person that plays the sport he hates the most.

What could go wrong? "Guys, I have an idea."

6

Jacks

I step out of the locker room ready to have a normal practice, when I notice a bunch of people off to the side of the rink. Coach told us there was some sort of surprise at today's practice, but I didn't expect a bunch of cameras and people to be sitting in the stands. I'm on the ice and doing some warm up laps when Grant comes up next to me.

He's been a bit more moody than usual lately, and I think it has something to do with Hadleigh tutoring him. He's been passing his quizzes and shit, but his long-term goal is to pass the midterm, which he's super nervous about. He's preparing for the worry he's going to have when midterms come up, but I think something else got under his skin too. Something else being in the form of black hair and skirts. Grant and Hadleigh got into it at the Hidden Bear the other night, and Grant practically declared war on the color pink. He said it was unrelated, but she was wearing a pink sweater, so she clearly has an effect on him. Even if he can't see it, I can.

He's definitely on his way to being fully whipped for that girl, but he won't listen to me when I try to bring it up, so he's going to have to figure that out on his own.

"Are you done pouting or what?" I ask him.

"Dude, I'm not pouting. I haven't been getting enough sleep lately, that's all."

Ah, deflection. "Yeah…right." I decide not to press

further because I don't know if I can handle a whole spiel about how everything he's been doing lately has *nothing* to do with Hadleigh.

Coach calls us over and tells us that we're going to be scrimmaging each other today to prepare for our upcoming game, and then he splits us all up. It's the lower classman versus the upperclassman, and everything starts off fine, until I notice a flash of familiar blonde hair up in the stands.

I should've known that she was here in the sea of cameras, but that still doesn't stop me from thinking about her the entire practice. I try to show off a little, and some of it works and some of it doesn't, but at least I don't fall on my face again.

The upperclassmen end up winning, but it was a tight game. It was only 1-0 by the end, and Coach compliments us for all of our hard work so far. We end practice after doing some more cycling drills, sprints down the rink, and some short passing drills.

A few minutes later in the locker room, I hear shouting coming from a few lockers down. I notice Grant hasn't come back to where his shit resides, so I go check out what's going on. Grant and Ryan seem to be having some weird staring contest right now, and before Ryan can say another word, I speak.

"You almost ready, G?"

Grant turns his head to mine. Fire is blazing from his eyes. What happened before I got here? I open my mouth to tell him to hurry up, and he storms past me, throws his clothes on, and leaves. I look back at Ryan, who's sporting a huge grin on his face. God, I hate this fucking kid. He's such an asshole.

"You should quit while you're ahead, Barnes. If you

made Grant mad, then you really fucked up. We need to be a team, asshole. Act like a good teammate, or I'll get Holt to deal with whatever's going on."

Grant has a pretty big head start on me, and I hope he's going back to our dorm to sulk, rather than somewhere else. I think he needs to talk some shit through or something, and I want to get a lay of the land before he completely shuts me out. He tends to do that when he's too stressed.

As I make my way out of the locker room, I run straight into someone who seemed to be standing right by the door. I catch the person's wrist to prevent them from falling, and when I do, I feel a volt of electricity shoot into my hand.

And when I finally see whose wrist I'm holding, I'm surprised. "Fuck. I'm sorry, Claire."

"It's okay. It was my fault, anyway. I was standing right behind the door." She can't meet my eyes, and the room suddenly feels charged with some weird energy right now. *Was she waiting for me?* No. There's no way. Maybe she's waiting for Justin. I know they're friends because of that one day in the dining hall. I realize I haven't said anything in a long time, and now I feel awkward as fuck.

"Well, I should—"

"Would it be possible if—"

We speak at the same time, and the two of us start laughing as we do it.

"You first," I say to her, and her cheeks flush. *Damn, that was cute.*

"Okay." She fiddles with one of the rings on her finger as she looks over at me and takes a deep breath before speaking again. "I have a weird proposition for you. Is there somewhere we can talk?"

What the fuck? "Uhhh, sure? Do you wanna go to the café?"

"Yeah, if you have time, of course. I know you're probably busy."

I think she's nervous because she keeps fiddling with different rings on her fingers. What could she have to talk to me about that could make her this way? I'm officially intrigued, but my mind is running through a thousand different scenarios right now, and none of them are helping me settle. "My schedule is never too busy for you, Claire. Lead the way."

Claire

As I sit down across from Jacks in a booth at the café, I realize how horrible of an idea this is. Why did I think I could do this? This is something that would happen in a movie or a book, but why did I think I could pull this off in real life? I feel like an absolute idiot. Here I am, about to tell a stranger about this dumb drunken plan that I hatched up, and even better, I'm dragging him into it with me—if he says yes. I won't blame him for saying no because when I say this plan out loud, I'm probably going to recant everything and beg him to forget I ever said anything.

"So...what was your proposition?"

Oops. I may have zoned out, but when I meet his eyes again, he looks weirdly content being here—even though I asked him in the shadiest way possible. "Okay, uh. Bear with me, because I'm not sure how to say this."

"That would require me knowing what *this* is, but

no pressure or anything." He jokes at me and I silently thank him for breaking some of the tension that I was feeling. He seems to be good at that—making me feel less on edge. I just hope he doesn't think I'm crazy after this.

"I need a fake boyfriend." Well, there's no going back now.

Jacks starts laughing and I immediately regret doing this. "I'm sorry. I thought you said you needed a fake boyfriend. Maybe I need to get my hearing checked."

"That *is* what I said. I need a fake boyfriend, and I think you'd be perfect for it." Jacks just stares at me for a few seconds and I swear I can see the wheels turning in his head. *Is this too much? Have I gone too far?* No. No, stay strong, Claire.

"Me? Perfect?" he questions and I nod at him. "Is there a reason you need a fake boyfriend? I thought you had a *real* boyfriend..."

"Ex-boyfriend," I affirm.

"Oh. Okay..." He trails off again and I'm mentally slapping myself for how I'm going about this.

"I only need you to do it for a few months..." I trail off, unsure of what to say.

"Okay...but why do you need my help specifically?"

"Oh, right. Sorry, I meant to get to that part." I chuckle a bit, suddenly feeling nervous at the fact that I'm about to trauma dump all over this guy that I've only talked to a handful of times. I take a deep breath before speaking. "My ex-boyfriend, Clay, broke up with me a few weeks ago on our three-year anniversary. I had all this stuff planned, but when he got to my dorm, he decided that he was no longer in love with me, or so he said. Around two weeks later—a few days ago—I found out that he was seeing someone new. While I was wondering what I did wrong, he was going out with someone new and acting like he was perfectly fine. The worst part is that I catered my entire future around Clay. We went to high school together, in Delaware, and he convinced me to follow him here for college so we didn't have to do long distance." I pause my story and look over at Jacks. His face is full of...something. I can't tell what, but he doesn't interrupt me as I keep talking.

"I agreed because he reassured me that everything was going to be fine. He was excited to grow together in a new place, and create new moments together, which turns out to be a year and a half full of memories before he decided that he no longer loved me. Granted, our relationship wasn't the best. When I look back at the past few months specifically, I feel like an idiot. The signs were all there. I was just too dumb to read them."

"Claire, don't say that." His tone catches me off guard.

"What?"

"You're not dumb."

"Maybe not dumb, but my rose-colored glasses were on. He gave so many signs, and I never read them. Now he's moving on with someone new, perfect, and worthy of his love, and I'm stuck here wondering if I'm unlovable." I swear I hear Jacks mutter something under his breath, but when I look at him, his mouth is still down turned in a frown.

"I'm sorry that happened to you...but where do I fit into this?"

"Clay plays baseball here, and he loves the sport. It's his passion, but I figured that if he gets to move on and flaunt it in front of me, I should be able to as well." I pause. "I'm too nice, way too nice. I tend to give people a thousand chances, even if they fuck me over more than once. I've always been the nice girl, the one who tries to please everyone around me because I can't stand the thought of people being mad at me. Clay always used to make fun of me for it."

"I never thought that could be a bad thing. Also, from what you've told me, Clay seems like a dick. I'm sorry to say this, but I'm glad he's gone from your life. You deserve better." He runs a hand through his hair and feigns a smile.

"Thanks. That's sweet of you." I pause, feeling my cheeks heat at the words Jacks just said. "Anyway, he plays baseball, but he *hates* hockey players, and the sport itself. He says it's too easy—which is hypocritical because he can't even skate—and that it shouldn't exist as a sport so —"

"Ohhhh, I see where this is going." He laughs. "You want to fake date me and make him jealous? You want him to feel what you did from him moving on so fast."

"When you say it out loud like that, it sounds insane. *I* sound insane for even asking you to help me with this."

"I don't think insane is the word I would use. It sounds like the plot of some sort of rom-com. Like *Just Go With It*..." I stare at him, dumbfounded that he just mentioned that movie. "It's this movie where Adam Sandler and Jennifer Aniston pretend they're fake divorced so—"

"I know the movie. I'm surprised that *you* know it."

"Claire, you better not be movie-shaming me."

"I'm not! I just wasn't expecting you to mention it...or know the plot..." I start to laugh, and so does he. This conversation seems really light, as if we had been friends forever and are just talking over a late-night coffee. It's weirdly easy being here and talking to him right now.

"I'm a big fan of rom-coms. My mom used to show me and my dad all of her favorites. I grew up watching them. Hence my advanced knowledge of them."

That's adorable. I feel like Jacks is the kind of person that will keep surprising me as I learn more about him. "I love that. I'm a big fan of Hallmark Christmas movies. The cheesier the better."

"Well then, I think we've just discovered the first thing we have in common." He smiles at me and my heart leaps in my chest.

"Does that mean you're agreeing to help me?"

"Maybe. Can I have a day or two to think about it?"

"Of course. I did just bombard you with all this shit, so I'm sorry. Also, if it helps, I thought of this plan while drunk off my ass with my friends. Sober me is unfortunately not that interesting."

"I don't know. I think she's fun. You deserve some payback, anyway. Plus, what kind of name is Clay, anyway? He sounds like a dick."

"He was okay…I guess. Every time I think back on things, my opinion changes. Most of the time, I end up pissed." I fiddle with my rings as I say that. The two of us are quiet for a few moments, and the silence becomes deafening as neither of us speaks. "You know he almost killed me once?"

Jacks looks visibly dumbfounded. "What?!"

"He forgot I had a peanut allergy, and he almost killed me." I laugh, thinking about it now because how was I so stupid? "That would've been the worst way to die. Death by dumbass boyfriend not remembering his own girlfriend's allergies."

"Well, good riddance to him, then. Though you should probably stop telling me things about him, or I might explode. This guy seems like the worst."

He kind of is the worst. I see that now. I think talking this out with someone outside of my friend group is helping because he's confirming all the things I've been thinking, but too afraid to say out loud. Clay was the worst, and I *do* deserve better. I'm about to speak when Jacks beats me to it.

"Are you asking anybody else to be your fake boyfriend? Or was it just me?"

"I had a few other options but—"

He cuts me off. "Don't ask them. I still need a second to think about this, but don't ask anyone else. Okay?"

"Okay, I won't. Just let me know by the end of the week? And don't tell anyone about...you know, the whole fake thing," I ask him, unsure if I was hearing jealousy in his voice or just imaging it. "Oh, and here's my number so you can text me your decision." I slide a piece of paper across the table and Jacks pockets it in his hockey hoodie.

"Sounds good." He smiles. Jacks smiles fully with his teeth, while Clay used to just turn his lips up. He's got a beautiful smile. "Shall we?"

"Shall we what?" I ask him, confused as to when he got up from the table.

"I'm walking you back to your place."

"Jacks, it's fine I—"

"Claire, we're not even fake dating yet. Please don't fight me on this and let me walk you back. It's dark out." Even though I barely know Jacks, this seems like a fight I'm not going to win, so I concede and nod my head.

"Good. Shall we?"
        "We shall."

7

Jacks

It's been two days since the girl I've liked since freshman year asked me to be her fake boyfriend. I've slowly been losing my mind. I've barely slept, and the worst part is that I can't tell anyone *why*.

Okay, well, I did tell my parents. They're not here, so I figured they would be good options to talk this out with. I told them my situation, how this girl I've always thought was beautiful asked me to fake date her to make her ex jealous. My mom said the same thing I did—that it sounded like the start to my very own version of *The Proposal* featuring Sandra Bullock and Ryan Reynolds, sans the green card aspect.

My dad was unsure if it was a good idea, but my mom was all for it.

Which left me in the same spot that I was in before.

How do I go into this knowing that if given the chance I would want this to be real, when I know she wants it to be fake? Maybe I should tell her the truth, but the thought of doing that scares me.

God, I'm such a coward. I thought I was being smooth as fuck last night, but I was just faking it until I made it. I put on my confident persona, and it seemed to work because I made her laugh a few times. She also told me a lot of vulnerable stuff, so that must mean that she trusts me, or else she wouldn't have shared that with me.

Right?

God, my head is so confused.

Do I tell Claire about my feelings, or do I continue to hide behind them like a coward and fake it with her until it ultimately ends?

If I tell her, she'll probably think I was a creep. If I don't tell her, then maybe as we fake date over the next few months, it'll eventually turn real for *both* of us.

I definitely know which way I'm leaning, but I'm too scared to take the leap. What happens if this all blows up in our faces? What happens if people find out we're not a real couple? What happens if Clay decides to come crawling back, and she gets back with him? Is that what she wants?

I'll have to ask her all these questions at some point, or maybe not. I don't fucking know. I don't want this to be fake. If it were up to me, I would've had the courage to say something to her in the first place, but the universe has decided differently. I have an opportunity to get to know Claire, and I *want* to know her. I want to know her favorite movies, and I want to memorize them so I can recite the words to her as we watch them. I want to know what makes her smile, laugh, and cry. God, I'm pathetic. I'm doing all of this for a girl who barely knows anything about me.

But you can change that by agreeing to her plan.

Fuck. Well, I guess there's my answer.

I pull out the slip of paper she handed to me last night with her phone number on it, and begin to type out a message. Grant walks into our dorm as I'm typing and sulks into his desk chair. We have practice soon, but he's been acting weird over these past few days. Every time I try to ask why he scoffs out some excuse and changes the subject to something random.

Hadleigh has gotten under his skin, and it's funny to see him all fucked up over it.

I finally type out a message, but my finger hovers over the send button for a few seconds as I overthink this decision for the thousandth time.

"Hey, G. Do me a favor," I say as I get off my bed and over to where he sits.

"What's up?"

"Press send on this for me."

"Why can't you do it? And whose number is this? There's no contact name or picture..." He trails off and looks at me with a weird stare. "Jacks, is this to your dealer? Do you have a dealer? I won't be involved in any illegal activity..."

"Grant, stop. It's to someone important. Can you just do it?" I ask him.

"Okay, but answer one question. Are you doing drugs?"

"No. Now press send for me before I ask someone else."

"Fine." He reaches out and clicks the button before I can stop him. "You're welcome."

"Thanks." I set her name in my phone, and place it face down on my desk.

Jacks: I'm in. When do we start?

Fuck. There's no going back now. I'm either the luckiest guy on the planet, or the stupidest. I pace in my room until I hear it ding again a few minutes later.

Claire: Great! How about Monday?
Jacks: Sounds good. Lunch in the dining hall? You know, so people can see us...

Claire: Perfect.

Jacks: Are we thinking soft or hard launch?

Claire: Oh my, okay now I'm laughing. You continue to surprise me, Jacks Moore. Looks like all those rom-coms paid off...

Jacks: Oh, for sure.

Claire: Hard launch, I think. Why not just go for it, right?

Jacks: Perfect. I'll bring you a jersey to wear.

Jacks: I think number 86 is gonna look good on you, Canes.

Claire: Me too. I can't wait, fake boyfriend.

Jacks: Me neither, fake girlfriend.

I lock my phone and feel myself smiling like an idiot. This is good, right? I think I'm doing okay so far, but I hope this doesn't end horribly.

I'd hate to ruin something before I ever fully had it for real.

8

Claire

As I sit across from Jacks in the dining hall, I'm acutely aware of all the eyes on us. I'm overthinking my own plan, but he seems calm, cool, and collected. Though his leg hasn't stopped bouncing since we sat down, so maybe he is nervous. If he is, I can't tell by his face or body language. We met up yesterday outside his place, and he gave me one of his jerseys to keep. It's a bit big, but with him being a lot taller than me, I should've known it would be. It also featured in my latest Instagram post, which shows Jacks taking a picture of me with my back to the camera, with the caption, '86 looks better on me.' You can tell it's him because the mirror in the picture shows his full silhouette.

Jacks did agree to a hard launch, and he even let me tag him. I don't have many followers, but this has already become my most liked post ever.

And it's only been one day.

I feel like I'm in over my head, but there's no going back now. This honestly excites me a little bit. I've never done something like this before. I've never been petty and wanted to make someone feel as bad as I did. It's refreshing in a way. It feels good not to be constantly tiptoeing around someone else's feelings because Jacks is always up front with what he feels. As far as I know—which isn't much—he doesn't make rash decisions, and I'm excited to get to know him more over the next few months.

My thoughts are cut off by the feeling of a hand in mine. When I look down at where it rests on the table, I notice that Jacks is mindlessly rubbing his thumb over my hand. It feels good, and I doubt he knows he's doing it because he's tapping away at his phone.

His hand feels nice in mine. It almost feels natural the way we do this. Even though we both know it's fake, I think it helps that it's so easy for us. We both might be nervous as hell right now, but on the outside, we just look like two people eating lunch together. Our two sandwiches remain fairly untouched because we both seem too nervous to eat.

"So, we should go over the rules for this arrangement," I say to him.

"Yeah, yes, of course. What sort of rules do you have in mind?"

"PDA is fine—my love language is physical touch—but for now stick to cheek kisses as we get to know each other."

"Noted." He smiles at me. "My love language is words of affirmation. What else?"

"I love that you know that." I pause before saying my next rule. "Don't fall in love with me," I say, and he just laughs.

"I didn't mean to laugh, this entire conversation reminds me of every fake dating movie ever. I just never thought—"

"Never thought you'd be living one in real life? Yeah, me neither."

"It is kinda fun, though. I won't fall in love with you, Claire. Unless you make me, and then that's entirely your fault."

My mouth falls open as butterflies erupt in my stomach. "Jacks Moore, I'm serious. It's too soon for me, and I wouldn't be able to give you what you deserve. I'm sure your last girlfriend was probably better for you, considering we're fake dating, so I'm sorry about all this."

"If she existed, she still wouldn't hold a candle to you, gorgeous. Trust me on that." His eyes meet mine, and I feel my heart start to race. *He's never had a girlfriend? Is that what he just said?* "What else?"

"Uh...I think that's it for me. What rules do you have?"

His eyebrows pull together as he thinks. "When you photograph my games, you wear my jersey. Between us, we're fake, obviously. But I want everyone on campus to know that you're mine. I want to flaunt you around as much as I can. Okay?"

My cheeks heat when he says that. Clay *never* used to have me wear his stuff. He always told me it was too dirty, or some other excuse. Jacks saying all of that is making me feel all sorts of things that are leaning into dangerous territory, but I brush it off for right now. "I'm okay with that."

"Good, and there's no timeline on this. I'm at your mercy, Claire. You tell me we're done with this, and we're done, okay? You have all the power here." Our eyes are locked, and I feel like he's staring right into my soul.

"Noted." *Why did hearing him say that to me feel as good as it did?*

Jacks then slides his phone over to me, and I pause, wondering what he wants me to look at. When I grab it, I see my contact profile up on his phone. "Uhhh, what's up?"

"I wanted you to add a picture and whatever you

want your name to be in my phone. I didn't want to do it for you in case you wanted something specific."

"Oh, okay." I open up the camera on his phone and take a few pictures. Most of the faces I make are stupid and silly, but I notice Jacks watches me the entire time with a huge smile on his face. I swipe back over to my contact and put the picture in. I keep my name the same, but I add a camera emoji next to my name, just because. Before I give him his phone back, something in my contact notes catches my eye. I scroll down to where it says "all things Claire," and notice that Jacks has a list of things about me in it, like little reminders.

My peanut allergy is in all caps, he's marked down that I love Hallmark Christmas movies, and he even noticed that when I'm nervous, I fiddle with the rings I always wear. My love language is also on the list.

My pulse thrums in my ears, as I look at one of the sweetest things anyone has ever done for me. The fact that he made sure to write down stuff that he knew was important about me is really nice of him. He's committed to this, and I don't know how I'll ever be able to thank him.

"Here ya go," I say as I hand his phone back, trying to make it seem like I didn't see any of that because I don't know if he wants me to know about it yet. Or ever.

But God, why does knowing he did something so small and simple for me make my stomach feel all weird? Maybe it's nerves, but I need to shake those off so this looks convincing enough.

"Thanks." He returns a smile and continues rubbing his thumb over my hand. He meets my eyes for a second and then stops when he notices what he's doing. "I'm sorry, was that too much?"

"No, no. It was good. It felt nice."

"Oh good, okay." He pauses before continuing with thumb. "So, what's your favorite Christmas movie?"

"Hmmmm…" I pause to think through this question. There are some movies I watch for comfort, some to make me laugh, and some just because they're cheesy and make me feel happy for an hour and a half. "I'm going to have to go with *A Very Merry Mix-Up*."

"I think I've seen that one before. It sounds familiar."

"It's my mom and I's favorite. We rewatch it every year around Christmas time because it's just so bad that it's good. We also like to shit on the husband because he was an asshole from the beginning, and practically a walking red flag."

"Is that the one where she goes to the wrong house but she thought it was the right one because they had the same last name as her fiancé?"

"Yup." It's insane that Jacks knows all this stuff about movies. I only said the name, and he knew what movie I was talking about. "So, what's your favorite rom-com?"

"*You've Got Mail*."

"Oh, a classic then. That's a good one. Is there a reason why it's your favorite?" I ask him, wanting to know where his love of it came from.

"It's the first one my mom showed me when I was little. It's her favorite movie of all time, and even though my dad hates movies, he always sits down to watch her favorites with us. I think that was when I first realized what love was. Sitting through a cheesy movie with the person you love, even though you hate it, because you love seeing them happy." He pauses before continuing, "I used to sit on our couch and watch my mom recite all the lines to the movie. She knew all of them because she had seen it so many times. One day, I looked over at my dad and he was staring at my mom awestruck as she recited them."

"That's really sweet. My dad would never do that for my mom, he physically cringes when something romantic comes on." My parents love each other, of course they do, but they show it in different ways. My dad always wakes up early, before my mom, to make sure her coffee is ready for her when she wakes up. They do things differently, but I guess that reaffirms the statement that love looks different for everybody. Love will *never* look exactly the same to you as it does to someone else.

Before Jacks can say anything else, his eyes flit to the door and his eyes drop slightly. I turn to look around, but he grabs both of my hands and shakes his head at me. *What?*

"He's here." Jacks doesn't even have to say his name because I already know who *he* is. I've also found that since agreeing to do this with me, Jacks refuses to say Clay's name—at least in the two days we've been fake dating he hasn't.

My mind starts to panic. "Should we do something? Oh God, Jacks why are we doing this? Everyone is going to see right through us. I don't know how I expected this to go—"

"Claire." I meet his eyes, and he gives me a soft smile. "It's just us, okay? He doesn't matter, nobody else matters. We're just two people eating lunch together."

I nod as I take a calming breath and squeeze his hand, letting him silently know that I appreciated what he said. He's right. Of course, he's right. God, how is he so good at this? I change the subject and try not to think about how nervous I am right now. "I know you're majoring in sports management but—"

A voice cuts me off. "Claire."

I don't even have to turn around to know who it is. *I guess this was bound to happen eventually...*

I paste on the fakest smile I can, and turn around to face him. "Clay." He looks...fine. I thought I was going to turn around and see a whole new version of him, but all I see is a coward. A coward who broke my heart, and left me for a girl that looks exactly like me, just a thousand times prettier. "It's nice to see you."

His eyes are piercing mine, and I can practically feel the anger seeping off him as he realizes who I'm sitting with. *Good.* He better feel like his heart just bottomed out of his chest. It's what he deserves. "Yeah, you too. How have you been?"

I hear Jacks grumble, and I realize that I have yet to introduce them. "I've been great. School's been taking up a lot of my time, along with this one over here." I point to Jacks. "Clay, you know Jacks, right? He's one of the starters for the hockey team this year."

Clay tenses his jaw, in anger, as he reaches his hand out to shake Jacks' hand. But Jacks doesn't move from his seat, he just smiles at him as I take a sip of water. "It's nice to meet you. You're on the intramural baseball team here, right?"

I choke on the water I was just drinking as I hold my laughter down. *Oh my God.* Clay looks tense as he lowers his hand, and tilts his head to the side, clearly annoyed. *This might be the best day of my life.*

"Varsity baseball, actually."

"Ohhhh, right. Sorry about that." Jacks smiles.

"It's no problem." Clay tries to play it off, but anyone could tell how pissed he is right now. He always shows his emotions through his face, and he's not doing a very good job at hiding that right now. While the two of them engage in some sort of stare off for dominance, Clay's new girl slides up next to him beside where he stands. *God, she's even prettier in person.* "Claire, this is Evangeline. Evangeline, Claire."

She smiles at me. "It's nice to meet you." *I bet.*

"Yeah, you too." I smile back at her.

"And you are?" she asks Jacks, but he's already packing up our stuff. He stands and has my backpack on his shoulder. *How did he grab that so fast?*

"Claire, we're going to be late for class." He comes around and makes it so that Clay and Evangeline have to move out of the way. Jacks pulls my chair out for me, and motions for me to get up. Butterflies erupt in my stomach at the simple gesture. *Damn, he's good at this whole fake dating thing.*

"Thank you, kind sir." I smile at him as I get up. When I look back at Clay, his teeth are clenched so hard that I can almost hear it from here. "Nice to meet you, Evangeline." She smiles at me. "Clay."

"Good to see you. I hope you're doing well."

"Oh, she's doing more than well. That I can promise you, Cole." Jacks smiles as he locks our hands together.

"*Clay.*"

"Right." He turns us away from *that* situation, and we calmly walk out of the dining hall hand in hand. When we get outside, the two of us burst out laughing.

"Oh my God! I was trying so hard not to laugh, but the intramural joke and you calling him by the wrong name was *hilarious.*"

"The look on his face was priceless," Jacks smiles at me, still holding onto my hand like it's the most natural thing in the world. "Do you feel any better?"

"Sort of." I glance over at him. "Thank you for doing this. It means a lot that you agreed to help me even though we don't know each other that well yet."

"Yet being the keyword. Don't worry, gorgeous. We have all the time in the world."

Gorgeous. "Jacks, he's not around anymore."

"And?"

"And you don't have to keep the charade up all the time," I say while trying to silence the tension in my gut. *What is wrong with me?*

"I know, but I'm doing it just in case. Who knows, Clay could have spies around campus trying to keep tabs on you." He looks over at me and winks, and I laugh as the two of us walk to class together. *Should I hold his hand?* No. This is all fake anyway, and it's our first outing.

Baby steps, Claire.

9

Jacks

"Jacks, I don't think he cares enough to spy on me," Claire tells me as we walk side by side to our class.

"I'd have spies around if I lost the prettiest girl on campus." I look over and notice that she's playing with her rings again. "Just saying." *Way to go.*

"Thanks." She pauses before continuing, "You know I'm not doing this so I can get him back, right?"

I look over at her. That was why I thought she was doing this. That was one of the main reasons I wasn't going to agree to be a part of this. I didn't want to go into this with my own ulterior motives knowing that she had one too. I feel like I should just tell her. But I'm worried about her reaction. *"Hey Claire, I actually agreed to this because I've had a crush on you since freshman year when I first saw you and fell over on the ice. The only reason I wanted to do this whole fake dating thing is because I'm hoping you fall as hard as I did. And maybe if you get to know me, you'll realize that I'm a decent guy and all I want is to make you smile."*

But I'll never admit that. Not out loud anyway.

I wish I could. I'm too damn scared to put myself out there like that. I've never felt this way before, and I don't know if it's the real thing, but how do you know if you're good enough? How do you know if you're worthy of feeling a certain way?

I don't fucking know.

"If you don't mind me asking, why are you doing this?"

"I'm not normally this type of person. I don't go out of my way to hurt people like this, but with Clay..." She pauses before continuing again, as if she's trying to get the right words out. "Clay broke my heart. He was a person who I loved, or thought I loved, and he broke me a little bit. I never understood how you could do that to someone you supposedly loved. How you can knowingly say something to them and know how it will make them feel. You know that you'll see on their face that their heart is breaking. I just...I thought he was my person. It turns out that I just saw what I wanted to see, and not what he was actually showing me."

"Oh." I don't really know what else to say. I can't say that I understand because I don't. I've never been in that type of situation before, but I want her to know that she deserved better than that. That she deserved better than him doing that to her. "I'm sorry. I can't imagine giving your all to someone who just wakes up one day and decides he's not in love anymore."

"It's okay, I think. This is helping."

"What?"

"This"—she points between her and I—"Us."

Us. "I'm glad. I'm also glad that he looked like he was in pain when he saw us. You didn't see his face when he walked in, but it was priceless."

"Part of me feels bad, but the new and improved me counts that as a win in my department." I see how she tries to hide the smile that's coming through her face, but I notice it before she returns to her normal expression. "I also just wanted to make sure that you know I'm not trying to get back with him. It would be unfair of me to ask you to do this if that was my end goal."

"But it's not."

"No, it's not. I'm moving onto bigger and better things."

"Good. I do have to say that this is quite fun." It is. I genuinely have a good time when I'm around her. It's only just begun, but God, it feels like I've known her forever. It feels like we're just old friends catching up on things we missed in each other's lives. It's just so...easy with Claire. To be me and not be afraid that I'm unworthy of my feelings. I'd settle for just existing around her when all of this is over. After all, she did just get out of her last relationship, and I would never want to rush her into anything if she wasn't one hundred percent sure that it was what she wanted.

"Fake dating me is fun? Good to know I haven't completely lost my spark after all this shit."

"Claire, I think it would take a lot to make you lose your shine. But I'm glad you're not letting him win. I'm glad you decided to give a bit of what you felt back to him. He deserves to know that what he did, though awful, didn't destroy you."

Her smile hits me in my chest. "Thanks, Jacks." God, the way she says my name drives me crazy. She drives me crazy. All of these emotions she makes me feel is confusing me, and the way the sun is framing her face right now makes her shine even brighter. *Fuck.*

I open the door to our building for her, and we both step inside and immediately head into the lecture hall. I make my way over to my seat and expect Claire to go to her normal one, but when I sit down, I feel her slide into the seat next to me.

"Is this okay?" she asks me.

"More than okay. It's perfect," I say as I lean over and kiss her on the cheek. One of our rules is only cheek kisses, but that was the first one we've ever had.

I guess sparks really do fly because just that simple touch of my lips to her cheek felt...different. I pull back feeling like I got struck by lightning in the best way possible. Fucking hell. I look down at Claire and see her fiddling with her rings again.

Did she feel it too? If she does, she doesn't say anything about it for the rest of class, and I'm stuck barely paying attention to our lecture because I can't get that kiss out of my head.

10

Claire

As Jacks and I walk hand in hand into our Thursday night class, I find myself not wanting to let him go.

It's not that I want to keep touching him, no, I just like the way it feels—our hands joined together. Jacks lets me sit down first—we sit next to each other when we have a class together now—and I notice that he doesn't pull to let go of me either.

The two of us are good at this whole fake dating thing. *Maybe that one kid in my English class can write a book about this someday...*

"Hey, I wanted to ask you something," Jacks says to me as I come out from my daydream of a Jacks and Claire inspired romance novel.

"Yeah, what's up?"

"Can you help me with the genetics worksheet that's due tomorrow? I haven't even started it but every time I look at it my head spins." Oh. For some reason I expected something much more serious.

"Yeah, of course, but you realize our class is tomorrow, and the worksheet is due then, right?"

To that he laughs. "Yes, I do. I was hoping we could have a study date after class. You know we never stay the full three hours."

He does have a point. Professor Holland always lets us out early because he hates how late classes here go just as much as we do. "Okay."

"Cool. Do you wanna go back to my place? We can study in the common area..." He trails off suddenly while running a hand through his hair. *Why is he nervous?*

"Yeah, that sounds good." I smile at him as our professor makes his way into the room and starts talking. At some point during class, Jacks and I's hands find each other again.

And neither of us pulls away as our professor continues talking.

An hour and a half later, Jacks and I have moved from sitting next to each other in class, to sitting across from each other in the common area of his dorm. What once was us holding hands in class, has now turned to intertwining our feet underneath the table.

"Okay so, this worksheet is on genetics, which is chapter eight of the textbook," I tell him as I flip the book open to the right page. "Thankfully this one has a word bank because the last one we did like this was difficult."

He nods in agreement. "Yeah, I'm glad we at least have one this time, but I swear these words look fake. Who the hell came up with the words 'intron splicing'?"

I laugh when he says that. "Technically, all words are made up."

"Huh," he says to himself. "I guess you're kind of right."

"Now, I think we should each fill out as much as we can and check each other's answers when we're done. Does that sound good?"

"Yeah, that's perfect." Jacks suddenly gets up out

of his chair and goes to his room. When he comes back, he has a blue speaker in his hand. "Do you mind if I play some music? I can't work when it's completely silent, it makes my head feel loud and then I can't concentrate."

"I don't mind at all. I'm not a fan of too much prolonged silence either. I also don't enjoy hearing my thoughts that much, so play away."

Jacks puts on a random playlist and I find myself humming along to some of the songs I know as I fill out the worksheet. I'm trying my best to concentrate on each step of transcription for prokaryotes and eukaryotes, but I keep getting distracted by Jacks' low hums.

Is it possible to be attracted to a voice? I keep imagining that deep voice between my—

Woah. *Woah.* Claire, chill the fuck out.

I'm going to blame this on the fact that I've been in a dry spell for the last six months. Clay and I stopped having sex probably around the time he fell out of love with me, and every time I tried to do anything remotely sexy, he always turned me down.

God, I was so stupid. All the fucking signs were there.

I shove all of those thoughts out of my head and return to the worksheet. A few songs later, Jacks and I wordlessly trade sheets and I circle the ones I think we should talk more about, and I assume he's doing the same for me.

I go to hand him his worksheet back after checking it over, and when our hands touch, we both drop the sheet as if it was on fire.

It sure felt like it was. Surely our hands touching wasn't the object of all that heat. There's no way it was, so yeah, let's blame the worksheet.

"Sorry. I might play hockey but I have butterfingers sometimes," he laughs nervously.

"I get it. I practically trip on my own two feet most of the time," I say while trying to dissolve some of the electricity in here. The two of us are silent for a few moments before we lock eyes from across the table.

My stomach does a few flips before the tension gets broken by someone else entering our space. "Candy Canes! What the fuck is up girl?"

I smile, happy to see a familiar face. "Hi, Grant. Jacks and I are having a study date."

Grant turns to face his friend, whose cheeks are all red, and smiles wide at an embarrassed Jacks. "How is my best friend treating you? It better be a good answer or I'll kick his ass for you, Claire."

"Grant, are you serious right now?" Jacks tries to shove him away, but Grant won't budge.

"He's the best. Don't you worry, Carter, you'll be the first person I tell if Jacks is being an idiot." Jacks just rolls his eyes at that statement, which causes me to laugh. I don't think Jacks has an asshole bone in his body. Grant too. These two seem like one of the good ones, and anyone would be lucky to have them as a partner.

"In all seriousness, I'm glad you two are together. This seems like a good match. Plus, you guys are adorable," Grant sits down next to both of us. "You guys are sitting here doing a worksheet and I swear I could feel the tension in the room when I walked in. It's like, thick as fuck, and you're just *studying* together."

Jacks and I look quickly at each other, and then instantly away. I assume it's because we're both embarrassed about that comment, but I think Jacks plays it off well. "Thanks, G. Now, can we get back to it or are you going to annoy us for the rest of the night?"

"Now Jacks, at least give me a few minutes to get to know Claire. You're dating this beautiful girl, yet I barely know a thing about her." Grant claps Jacks on the shoulder and then turns to me. "So, tell me about yourself, Candy Canes."

"Well, I love Christmas movies—"

"WOW! You two are perfect for each other. Christmas movie lover meet rom-com movie lover. Now just that fact alone could make for a pretty good storyline. You guys should call the Hallmark channel or something."

"Grant, you just cut her off. Let her speak before you jump in," Jacks puts his hand up so Grant won't hear him, even though he's sitting right next to us both. "Sorry, when he gets excited about something he doesn't shut up about it."

I put my hand up too. "It's fine. It's nice that one person is excited to get to know me."

"He's not the only one, gorgeous." With that Jacks winks at me and I swear my stomach drops.

I turn back to Grant. "You already know that I love photography, but my favorite kind of pictures are candid. I think there's something special about capturing something that you didn't mean to. Those are often my favorite pictures that I've taken."

Grant's face lights up when he hears that. Damn, Jacks was right. Grant *does* get excited at basically everything. I've never seen someone smile this much. "Can you shoot a candid right now? I want to see the master at work."

"Grant, come on—"

I cut Jacks off. "Babe, it's fine." *That slipped out*

easily. "Give me something to shoot, and I'll gladly do it."
I take my phone out of my bag and flip to my camera. I
don't have my good camera, but this will do for now.

Grant looks around for a moment before his eyes
narrow. "How about Jacks here? He'd be a good subject for
candids since he probably gave you one of the best ones
that first day."

"Grant, no I'm sure there's something else—"

"I mean I don't want to make him uncomfortable
—" The two of us are stuttering through our sentences
before Grant shakes his head at us.

"Claire, you said to give you something. So I am.
Jacks is a wonderful subject." Grant smiles. Does he know
we're faking it, or is this a test?

"He is." I look at Jacks from across the table. "Are
you okay with this?"

He only appears *slightly* uncomfortable, but he
nods his head. "As long as you're the one behind the
camera, I know I'm in good hands."

"That's the spirit!" Grant says as he gets
comfortable in his chair.

"Where and how do you want me, Claire?"

Why are my legs tingling all of a sudden? This might
be harder than I thought. "We can just start like this."

He nods at me, and I start to shoot him from
different angles, but nothing feels right. The lighting, the
angle, the poses. I need to get him to loosen up, but this
whole situation is just...awkward. After a few minutes,
an idea pops into my head. "Hey, Grant? Can you turn on
the *You've Got Mail* playlist on Apple Music?"

"You've got it!" I laugh at the obvious pun he just
made, and then turn to Jacks.

"You're too stiff. Loosen up a bit, babe. There's

nothing to be afraid of."

"I just don't know what to do with my hands! I feel weird sitting here all eyes on me."

The music starts, and another idea pops into my head. "Grant, tell some jokes or something. Make us laugh. You're pretty good at that, and Jacks—"

"Yes, gorgeous?"

I pause for a second and let that phrase hang in the air. "Go sit on the couch over there. I can't see enough of you on the chair."

He does what I say, and the next half an hour is one of the most memorable times I've ever had. Jacks loosens up, Grant makes *all* of us laugh our asses off, and eventually I'm the one in front of the camera and Grant is taking candid photos of all of us. By the end, the three of us have laughed so much that we're all sitting on the couch and looking over the photos we all took—while pointing out the best shots that we got.

"Well Claire, it looks like Jacks was right," Grant says to us.

"Right about what?" I ask as I lightly tap Jacks on the arm—to which he smiles, but it's not a big deal.

"He told me that you were phenomenal behind the camera, and of course I knew that because of the hockey photos, but I like how you capture the normal aspects of life—like laughter and happiness."

Jacks told Grant I was phenomenal behind a camera? "Well, thanks. Tonight was really fun. Thank you, guys, for doing that for me."

"Doing what?" Jacks asks me.

"Reminding me why I fell in love with photography again."

Grant knocks my shoulder and I fall into Jacks. "No

problem, Candy Canes. I can't wait to print out some of these and hang them on our wall. Do you guys think I'd make a good model?"

To that, the three of us laugh again, and I find myself smiling more than I ever have with these two guys at my side.

Oh, how the times change...

Three Days Later

Jacks: Hello m'lady. This is me requesting a formal first fake date for this Wednesday night after my practice.
Jacks: Are you free perhaps? I'd love to flaunt you where everyone can see...
Claire: Oh my God, this is hilarious.
Jacks: Thanks?
Claire: I'm free. What kind of dinner are we thinking? Fancy?
Jacks: Not too fancy. Grant gave me the name of this Italian place in town. I thought we could just go there.
Claire: Tell Grant that he did good. Italian food is always the way to my heart.
Jacks: Noted. I'll keep that in mind for the future.
Jacks: Also, I'm glad you said yes because I already made reservations.
Claire: Then why did you ask me?
Jacks: Communication is one of our rules, unless you forgot Claire...
Jacks: Seems that only some of us can remember them...
Claire: I do remember them! But I'm starting to think this would be easier without rules...
Jacks: ???
Claire: Kidding.
Claire: I'm excited! This is my first real date in a while.
Jacks: What???? Didn't Clay take you out?

Claire: Not toward the end. I don't think we went on a proper date for the last six months of our relationship. He was always too tired or too something to go out.

Jacks: I'm gonna need you to stop telling me about him because the more I learn, the more I want to smack him and scold him for how he treated you.

Claire: Sorry.

Claire: Would it make you feel better to know that even though we're fake dating, you're definitely better than him already?

Jacks: ...

Jacks: Maybe...

Claire: Well, you are, just so you know.

Jacks: Oh, well, good. I'll pick you up after practice Wednesday?

Claire: Sounds good :)

Jacks: Wear something orange.

Claire: Orange????

Jacks: It makes your eyes pop.

11

Jacks

"Grant, I swear to God if you don't move, I'm going to kill you. I'm gonna be late." When Grant and I got back to our room after practice, he started acting weird as hell. Now, as I'm trying to leave to go pick up Claire for our first official fake date, he's standing in front of the door and blocking my path.

"Jacks, I'm not letting you leave until you tell me where you're going. I want to know more about you and Claire. Besides that one night last week, you've been a closed book about you two."

I should've known this was going to happen. Since taking our fake relationship public, I forgot to tell my close friends any details about how this happened. Of course, my best friend was bound to have questions. I can't tell him it's fake, but I also feel weird lying to him. What do I do? "Yeah. Sorry, we've decided to keep things mostly private, you know?"

"Buddy! What the fuck?" He smacks my arm, hard.

"Ow! What the hell was that for?"

"I'm your best friend! You should know you can tell me anything and everything!" He paces around our room as if I just gave him life-changing news. God, he's so dramatic sometimes. Claire and I literally hung out with him the other day. I shouldn't have to explain every detail to him when he's seen firsthand that we're together.

At least to everyone else we are, but for us it's

"fake."

"You're the one being all hush hush about you and Hads. Care to comment on that, or are we going to ignore the giant elephant in the room?" *Yeah, two can play this game, jackass.*

"Don't fucking call her that, and fuck you."

"Mhm, whatever." He looks pissed and a little frustrated, and I instantly feel bad for bringing it up. That was shitty of me, but Grant just changes the subject. "Is that where you're headed? To see her?"

"Yes, we're going on a date. Can you move so I can leave and not keep her waiting?"

"If you had said that in the first place, I would've cleared a path for you! Go! Go! Go!" Grant claps his hands, and that gets me moving out of the building and into the night.

After I knock on her door, I wait until I hear her shuffling around and the door opens.

Nothing could've prepared me for this. She looks... I don't even think I have words to describe her beauty right now. Fuck, I'm not strong enough for this. She's wearing a burnt orange dress, short black heels that bring her height to just under my chin, and her normal rings and jewelry that she always wears. I noticed that she never changes her jewelry up, and I make a mental note to get her a new ring or necklace to add to her collection— gold, of course, so it matches the rest. Our clothes match, but only a little bit. I'm wearing a brown polo, black slacks and some dress shoes. Grant told me the place was semi-fancy, and this was all I had.

Or maybe that's too weird? I don't know, but all I *do*

know is that Claire looks like a fucking goddess tonight.

She waves her hand in front of my face and smiles at me. "Jacks? Are you in there?"

"Yeah, I'm sorry. Just...stunned, I think."

"Stunned in a good way? I can change if it's too much. I was worried that it would be."

"You look beautiful, Claire. Truly...it just caught me off guard for a second."

"Careful, Jacks. Any more of that will make me think this isn't fake."

God, I could say right now that it doesn't feel fake, but I refrain. "Good one," I say, trying to play off what I feel right now. "Are you ready to go, gorgeous?"

"I'm ready," she smiles, and I swear I feel it in my chest. It feels good making her smile. I hold my arm out for her, and she wordlessly loops hers through mine as we make our way toward my car.

Claire

The car ride to the restaurant was full of me badgering Jacks about his music taste, and him and I agreeing that Taylor Swift is one of the best musical artists of all time. The conversation came up because his playlist had songs from *Fearless* on it, and when I asked him how he knew all the words to *Hey Stephen*, he just scoffed at me and laughed—as if he *wouldn't* know them.

Needless to say, I was impressed. Clay never liked listening to music...like at all. It was honestly kind of weird. I feel like that's an odd trait to have. Clay also never liked dancing with me. Even when we went to prom together during our senior year of high school, he barely slow danced for one song until his friends stole him away.

Knowing Jacks is a Swiftie immediately makes me trust him more. A lot of guys would pretend to be a fan just to seem like they have something in common with you. Not Jacks. He was fully belting the words to *Mr. Perfectly Fine* on our way here, after he dedicated it to Clay. It fit my situation almost *too* well, and we both got a good laugh about it. It's not that I didn't trust him before, but this just solidifies the fact that he continues to surprise me in the best ways possible. Who knew Jacks had so many layers underneath that introverted, shy personality of his?

We've been sitting at our table for a few minutes, and I have to say that this is the most fun I've had in a while with someone of the opposite gender. It almost feels a bit *too* easy, and I'm scared that something is going to ruin this. Our friendship, of course. I could see us being friends after all this fake dating stuff is over. It sounds really nice—being friends with him. It feels right, like we just fit like two puzzle pieces. Two *friendship* puzzle pieces.

"So, besides hockey, have you ever played any other sports?" I ask, wondering if he's spent his whole life at the rink, or if it took a second to get there.

"It's just been me and the ice since I was a kid, and I wouldn't have it any other way." He smiles at that, and I can tell he's thinking of his fondest memories from the past. He's got a few different types of smiles. The genuine one which lights up his whole face, the awkward one where only one part of his mouth upturns, and the nervous one where he tilts his head down. I don't know how I know the difference between them, but I do. It's easy to tell, and he's fairly easy to read. "What about you? Have you played any sports?"

"No. When I was growing up, my dad would watch sports all the time, and when I was little, I used to sit on his lap while he explained the rules to me. That's how I got into sports, and eventually into sports photography."

"Wow, I love that. My parents were the ones who put me into hockey because of how much energy I had as a kid. I've thanked them profusely since, because hockey is...everything to me. I know it's just a sport, and it might sound insane, but—"

I cut him off. "No, it doesn't. It's cool that sports and things like that are able to make us feel so whole. That's what photography does for me. I love seeing how I can capture different things in just the split second that it takes for a photo to be taken."

"Yeah, yeah. It's exactly like that. The rush I get from hockey is just so different from anything else. I feel like a completely different person when I'm on the ice."

"In what way?"

"More confident, I think. I know what my job is when I'm out there, and I'm confident in my skills and ability to get it done. I've never really felt like that in normal life." He smiles sadly, and before I can ask him what that means, our waitress comes up.

"Hello and welcome. I'll be your server tonight! My name is Cassie," she says as she sets some breadsticks down on our table. "Do you need a few more minutes, or are you good to order now?"

I look over at Jacks, and he nods his head. "I think we're ready now. Ladies first."

"I'll have the—"

"Wait, Claire, just before you order," he turns to the waitress. "Do you guys have or use anything that involves peanuts or peanut oil?"

Oh my God. Did he really just ask her that for me? "No. We're a completely nut-free establishment."

"Great. Thank you so much." He points his hand at me, as if motioning me to continue. I suddenly don't know if I can because him asking that one question just threw my head for a loop. *Clay never did that.*

"I'll have the chicken parmesan, please." My voice shakes a little as I order because I feel so...well I don't know what I feel, but the butterflies in my stomach have woken up.

Jacks closes his menu. "I'll have the same, please."

Cassie collects our menus and walks away, leaving us in a weird silence as the two of us sit across from each other.

"Thank you for doing that," I say to him.

"Doing what?"

"Double-checking with the waitress over my allergy. That was really thoughtful of you." *And nobody has ever done that before for me because I'm normally the one who has to do it, and now I feel all weird inside because that might be the sweetest thing anyone's ever done for me.*

"Of course. You can never be too careful, especially with food allergies." He throws his awkward smile at me before he reaches over and grabs my hand. He rests our hand in the middle of the table before speaking again. "I know it's important to you that I remember that, and trust me when I tell you that it's easy to remember everything about you because of who you are. You're a great person, Claire. I'm glad to be able to get to know you, even if our relationship is supposed to be fake. I'm happy that parts of it can just be for us, and not everybody else."

Oh. "Me too. You're a lot different than I thought you would be, Jacks Moore."

"Right back at you, gorgeous." There he goes again, slipping that nickname out so easily.

"What did you mean earlier when you said you feel more confident on the ice than you do in real life? I don't mean to press, but you seem so put together all the time." It's hard to imagine Jacks like that. Sure, he's pretty shy, but I would *never* describe him as nervous or unsure of himself.

"I didn't mean it like that, I just...I don't know. I've never had a relationship like you and Clay did. I've never felt the feeling of being in love with someone, and I guess I just feel like I've missed out on this huge thing, and part of me is scared that I'm never going to feel what it's like—to love someone and have them love me back the same amount. I've had small relationships, one to three months, but I never felt anything during those. Not the butterflies, not the silence that comes with feeling in love with someone feels like, and not the crazy urge to lose my mind over the thought of losing the person that I love."

Wow. Now that he describes it like that, I'm not sure if I've ever felt it either. Clay was my first boyfriend, and even being a senior in high school, I felt like I was always behind my friends in the dating department. When I finally got with Clay, it just felt right. It was easy. But when I lost him, it didn't hurt as much as I thought it did. I didn't even cry until a few days later, but that might've just been me missing the feeling of having a person by my side, of knowing that he was there.

Was I even in love with him? Every time I look back over the past three years, I come up with more questions that I can't answer. I don't know. I don't know if I ever really loved him, or if his love was just convenient for both of us.

"That was beautiful."

"Thanks," he smiles at me. *A real one.*

I'm about to respond when I hear a familiar laugh from across the restaurant. *No. There's no way he's here right now.* But when I turn my head to look around, I spot him almost immediately. I sigh heavily as I turn back to Jacks and find him following where my stare just was. When he spots Clay with his new girlfriend a few tables over, I see him visibly tense as he sits across from me. I can't tell if he's annoyed that we seem to keep running into him, or just pissed off that he's breathing the same air as my shitty ex that he doesn't like.

"Do you wanna leave? We can go somewhere else," he asks me that while caressing his thumb over my hand.

"No. It's okay." I'm not going to let Clay ruin another night. He doesn't get to do that.

"Are you sure? We can always go spray paint his car, or slash his tires..."

"I'm positive. Ignore him, it's just us," I say as I laugh at what he said and squeeze his hand in mine.

A few minutes and some light conversation later, our food comes and we eat. This place actually has really good stuff. Maybe Jacks and I can come here again and try something different next time. Clay doesn't come over to us. I doubt he even knows or cares that we're here, and the rest of the night is actually pretty wonderful. I've laughed a lot tonight, and I find myself feeling really carefree with Jacks. Normally when Clay and I went on dates, I was too hyperfocused on how I was acting to be able to enjoy it. God forbid I embarrass Clay in public, but with Jacks, I don't really care. I laugh as loud as I want, I smile, and I'm not as worried when I'm with him. It feels good to let loose and just exist for once. I like it. When the check comes, Jacks tries to grab it before she even sets it down, but he's too slow.

"Claire," he says my name and I feel goosebumps spread all over my body.

I hold his stare. "Jacks."

"I asked you out, therefore I'm paying."

"Consider this a thank you for all you're doing to help me," I say, hoping that he'll drop it.

"It's the right thing to do, especially when you ask a beautiful girl out to dinner." He's still drilling his gaze into mine.

"Jacks, please just let me."

He's quiet for a few seconds. "No." And then he grabs the check from me while I'm caught off guard, and slips his card into it.

"That's unfair."

"Don't fight me on this, gorgeous." He runs a hand through his hair. "You're not going to win."

"Fine," I say as Cassie comes to pick up the check from us. I look out the window and notice that it's started to rain. I'm not worried about my outfit or anything, but it's dark out, and I normally hate driving in the rain. "I didn't know it was forecasted to rain tonight."

Jacks turns his head and looks out the window. "Me neither. We'll be okay. I can always pull the car up."

"But then you'll get wet."

"So?"

"If you're getting wet, then I am too. It's only fair." Jacks laughs when I say that, and I immediately regret speaking when I hear it out loud. "Oh, come on. You know what I meant."

He continues to laugh as I shove my card back into my purse, and I feel him come over and pull my chair out for me. The two of us exit the restaurant and stand in the entry way.

"Do you want to run, walk, or just say fuck it and dance?" he asks me as I feel some raindrops fall onto my face.

Dance? "What the hell are you talking about? You want to dance? Right now?" He's got to be joking, right? There's no way he's being serious.

"Unless you don't want to..." He trails off while running a hand through his hair. I find myself not wanting to say no to him right now.

"Fuck it. Why not?"

As soon as I say that, he grabs my hand and pulls us into the rain together. He pulls me into his chest before he swings us around. I can almost hear song lyrics in my head as this spontaneous dance in the rain occurs. We separate for a few seconds and dance by ourselves. *This feels good. I feel good.* This moment of spontaneity has solidified itself in the spot of one of my all-time favorite moments. It feels good to let go and let the rain wash all my worries out of me, even if for just a few seconds. I've always loved that about the rain. The world always feels brand new after rain falls and the clouds go away.

Jacks twirls around in the rain as he saunters back over to me. I'm standing in the same spot because I'm too captivated in this moment to be able to move my feet. He grabs my hands from where they hang at my sides and immediately starts to swing me around in his arms. I can feel the rain falling onto my face, and it feels good. Refreshing almost. The two of us are smiling and laughing our asses off as we dance in the rain like nobody's watching. Droplets drip from the ends of Jacks' hair, and he runs his hand through it as if that will fix it.

It's a mess, but seeing the smile on his face is worth it all.

I spin away from him and lift my arms out, feeling the rain on my skin while it drips down my face. I'm *drenched,* but I've never had this much fun before. When I lock eyes with Jacks, he holds his hand out, and I walk over and give mine to him. He immediately pulls me into him and I look into his hazel eyes, droplets falling from his hair, smile on his face, and I suddenly want him to kiss me.

Woah. Where did that come from? The two of us stand like statues in the parking lot, neither of us wanting to break this moment apart. I find myself dragging my hand through his hair, and his head leans back when I do that. *Fuck.* Why was that so hot?

"Claire..." he starts to say, until someone comes and shoves us apart. Jacks falls back to the pavement and when I try to rush over and help him off the ground, an arm stops me.

"What the fuck are you doing?" Clay yells at me through the rain.

Oh fuck no. "That's none of your goddamn business, Clay!" I look around and see Evangeline standing underneath the restaurant, staying dry while letting Clay do whatever the hell he's doing right now.

"It *is* my business. We broke up weeks ago, and you're already whoring it up on campus with a fucking hockey player? I thought you were better than that, but I guess I dodged a bullet when I broke up with you."

"I could say the same for you. Unless Evangeline is just another girl you're going to 'fall out of love' with after three years. She deserves better than you. *I* deserved better than you, and I found it. Leave me the fuck alone." God, this feels good—yelling at him in the rain.

Clay smiles at me. "I have no regrets about the past few months."

I can't say that doesn't sting, especially since I gave so much of myself to him only for him to turn around, use me, and then break my heart. "You saying that is such bullshit! Why would you be out here breaking up my date if you supposedly have no regrets? Lying doesn't look good on you, Clay. I think you just want things that you can't have. Is that what happened with us? Is that what's going to happen when someone else piques your interest over her? You're the one stuck in a never-ending cycle of bullshit, and when I move on without you, you get pissed." I pause, silently applauding myself for finding my voice. "Fuck off, and leave me alone. You don't dictate my life anymore. I do."

I go over to where Jacks is sitting on the pavement and hold my hand out to him. He smiles, takes my hand, and stands up.

"Some guy to have by your side if he can't even stand up for you. I bet he'll just take what he wants from you, and then drop you like all those hockey players do."

Jacks just stands next to me, laughing and shaking his head. "If you knew Claire, you would know she doesn't need me to speak for her."

"Oh yeah, I know Claire real well, pretty boy. I know just how tight her—" Clay isn't able to get the rest of those words out because before I know it, Jacks raises his fist and punches him square in the jaw.

Jacks stands there shaking his hand off and wincing in pain. *Has he ever done that before?* "Don't fucking talk about my girlfriend like that."

My girlfriend. God, why did that sound so good coming from his mouth? Jacks grabs my hand, opens my car door for me, and before I know it, we're speeding off into the night like we're in a getaway car or something. A few minutes of silence later, I look over at him driving with a smirk on his face.

Then we burst out laughing. Like fully belly laughing.

We don't make small talk as we drive back to campus, but when he finally gets back to the lot, neither of us moves to get out of the car. I take in the state of us. Jacks and I are soaking wet, our clothes ruined. His knuckles have bruises forming on them, and I see a few scrapes on his elbows from when Clay pushed him. *God, what a fucking asshole.* How did I not see it before? How was I so blind to the fact that Clay is clearly not a good person?

I feel some adrenaline running through my body from the past few hours. Tonight was *crazy*. Not only did I have a great time on our date, but Jacks and I danced in the rain. I wanted to kiss him. And then all the stuff with Clay...it's been a weird night.

But why do I find myself wishing it wasn't over? That was the most fun I've *ever* had with someone. I'm the first one to break the silence. "Is your hand okay?"

I can see his jaw clench from here as he tries to play it cool. "It's fine."

"Jacks. Let me see it."

He looks over at me before gently moving his hand to sit in mine. I brush my other hand softly over his knuckles. He winces a bit, but I don't think he broke anything. "You need an icepack."

"Claire, I'll be fine."

"Jacks Moore, you're a hockey player and you need to use your hand. Promise me that you'll ice it tonight."

He just laughs. "What?"

"Even when you're yelling at me and using my full name, you still look adorable," he smiles at me. "Are you cold?"

"A little. I'll be good in a few if you turn the heat on full blast," I say to him. As I click one of the vents open, I feel something against my arm. When I look over, Jacks is holding onto one of his hoodies.

"Put it on, Claire."

"Jacks, no, I'm fi—"

"You're shaking. Please. Just wear it," he says, shoving the hoodie into my lap.

"Seriously, I'm okay. We're not far from campus." I expect him to argue with me, but instead he grabs the hoodie, yanks it over my head, and practically forces me to wear it. I shove my arms through the sleeves and my body starts to warm up. "Thanks."

"I've got to keep my girl warm. I don't want you getting hypothermia. I wouldn't be a good fake boyfriend if I let that happen."

Here come the fucking butterflies again. I don't know if it's the adrenaline from tonight, or the fact that he stood up for me earlier, but I find myself wanting to kiss him again.

So, I do.

I lean over the center console and press my lips to his. He's shocked for a moment, but then he finally kisses me back with the same ferocity that I am.

And holy fuck, can he kiss. His right hand comes around and cups my neck, and I feel him wince when he does that. "We should stop," I mumble into his mouth.

"Yeah, you're right. We should." But neither of us does. Jacks keeps kissing me and I keep letting him, even though we're breaking one of the rules we set up at the beginning of this.

Cheek kisses only. But I don't want him to stop. I don't want to stop kissing him. *Fuck.*

"Jacks," I breathe against his mouth.

"God, Claire, don't say my name like that right now."

"We're breaking our rules," I say while still kissing him.

Jacks slips his tongue into my mouth, and I let him. He grabs me and pulls me on top of him, while simultaneously moving his seat back to make room for both of us. *Fuck, that was hot.* "Gorgeous, I'd break all the rules just to keep kissing you."

"Then don't stop."

"Whatever you say." And then his mouth is on mine again, and I can't think straight. My body is on fire as he cups my face, runs his hands down my back, and grips the back of my neck so he has better access.

"Is this okay?" I nod at him. "I need the words, Claire."

"It's more than okay."

When we finally pull apart half an hour later and go our separate ways for the night, I find myself questioning if this relationship is really as fake as I thought it was.

12

Jacks

I'm walking back to my dorm after my class just ended and I can't stop thinking about my car.

Correction, I can't stop thinking about what happened in my car two days ago. Two goddamn days. And all I can think about is the way she fucking tasted. I practically memorized the way her mouth felt, the curve of her jawline, and every fucking freckle on her face as she looked at me with those blue eyes that I want to drown myself in.

I truly haven't been able to focus the past few days. All because of what Claire and I did that night. *She* fucking kissed *me*. After we had a really nice dinner and danced in the rain together. Oh, and after I punched her shitty ex-boyfriend for running his mouth and trying to keep his leash on Claire.

That guy is a fucking asshole. I'm normally not one for violence, and I knew Claire could handle herself when it came to him. But when he started saying that fucking sentence, something in me just snapped.

He doesn't get to talk about her like that. He doesn't get to talk about *my girlfriend* like that, not if I'm around. Even if we are technically fake, she's still my girlfriend to everyone else.

Are we though? Fake? I knew it wasn't fake for me since the beginning—I hoped it would become real—but I'm starting to think it's not so fake for her either. For one, she broke the rules. Our rules. And she kissed me. It's been a struggle for me only being able to kiss her on the cheek because the first time I did, I felt like I got lit on fire.

I feel like I'm screwed. When I actually tell Claire how I've felt about her after all this is over, she's probably going to hate me. This whole fucking situation is so out of the ordinary, and I hate that I can't talk to Grant about it. Not that I could lately because of how busy he is denying his feeling for Hads. It's *very* obvious, at least to me, that he feels something for the girl. Anyone with eyes could tell.

I finally reach my dorm, and when I get inside, I plop onto my bed, feeling defeated and confused. I mindlessly reach for my phone so I can call my parents. They know about this whole situation but I haven't updated them in a while, and I could use some advice right now. They pick up on the third ring, and I see their faces fill up the screen of my iPhone.

"Hi, honey!" My mom smiles at me.

"How's it going, son?" My dad waves at me from the background and then turns to continue doing whatever he was doing.

"Hi, guys."

I'm from North Carolina, so I'm not too far away from home, but I still find myself missing my parents a lot. I'm an only child, so it's been weird for them too. They tell me all the time how quiet it is, and part of me feels bad, but the other part is glad to get some space. "Dad, how's the Firebird?"

"It's getting there. It's taking a little longer than I thought because I can't find some of the parts I need, but it's keeping me busy."

"That's good, not the parts things, but that it's

coming along." My dad loves fixing up old cars. He's done it ever since I was a kid, and I think he was secretly hoping that I'd like doing it too, but I got my mom's hobbies—romance books and romantic comedy movies. He was never disappointed in me though, he knows cars are like rocket science to me. I'm clueless when it comes to anything involving cars, but I still ask him about it and let him explain things to me because I like hearing how passionate he is.

"So...honey. How is everything?" I can tell from my mom's tone that she's *really* asking about how my own personal movie is going. I don't really know where to start, so I just tell them everything that's happened in the past few days. By the time I'm done, my dad has officially moved into the frame, and my mom has a huge smile on her face.

"You guys need to back up from the camera. You look strange." I laugh at them trying to crawl through the screen, and they move the phone back.

"Honey, she kissed you. I think that answers all your questions. She clearly doesn't think it's fake anymore..." My mom trails off as she looks over at my dad.

"Yeah, but how do I bring this up? We need to talk about it, but I don't know how to do that without telling her that I've liked her this whole time. She *just* got out of a relationship, and I don't want to make things weird or just be her rebound. I want something *real*."

"J, just have a conversation. It might be hard, but this girl seems special to you, and I know if I was you, and your mother was Claire, I'd not stop until she knew how I really felt. Just trust your gut and trust that she'll listen to you when the time comes. Even if you have to give her a little space, which she might need, trust that it will all work out." My dad smiles and raises a wrench at me before heading back to the car.

"Jacks, honey, that was good advice, but you definitely don't want to scare her away. Only you will know when the right time to talk to her about this is. Don't rush it. Sometimes you have to enjoy good things while they last, because one day you'll long for more of those moments. But please keep me updated. It's cool being able to experience a rom-com in real life!" My mom smiles.

"I will. I love you guys."

"We love you too, honey. Don't forget to tell Grant that we say hi!"

I laugh before answering. "I will." Grant's mom is like my second mom, and vice versa. My mom hangs up the phone and I have to say that I do feel a little bit better about this whole thing. I'm glad I was able to talk it out loud with people. My head was going crazy with all this information just floating around in there.

I grab my bag from the floor and am pulling out my homework to do when Grant walks in to our room. He looks...weird.

"Are you okay?"

"Jacks, don't ask me that right now."

I sigh heavily, knowing that my homework will have to wait. "What happened?"

"It's Hades and Ryan."

"What about them?"

"Get comfy. I have a lot to say." I do as he says and settle in as he jumps onto his bed and starts talking.

Whipped motherfucker.

Claire

"Guys, none of this is helping!" I yell at my two best friends while they laugh their asses off.

"I gotta say, I didn't see this coming." Sara laughs.

"I mean, he's hot, and he's nice. It was inevitable." Jess shrugs.

"UGH!" I say as I slump down onto my bed. It's been two days since I made out with Jacks in his car, and I've been spiraling ever since. I told these two that it's starting to feel real to me, and they just started laughing at me. "You guys are supposed to help me, not laugh."

"Why do you need our help? Just tell him!" Jess says to me.

"I can't! Do you even hear yourself? That sounds insane! Jacks is going to think I'm the craziest girl in the world."

"Yeah maybe, but you're the one who told us that he kissed you back, so it seems like he's feeling the same thing that you are babes." Sara tells me, and damn she's not wrong.

"But how can I jump right into something with Jacks when I just got out of a three-year relationship with someone I thought I loved? Isn't that too soon?" God, I'm so confused. Part of me is scolding myself because *of course* this would happen to me. Of course, I would fall into something real with a guy I only promised to fake date to make my ex feel like shit. And it worked for a second, but now, it's too much, too complicated. How do I trust that Jacks is in this? How do I trust myself? How do I trust that he's not going to just up and leave in the future when he eventually falls out of love with me? "Shouldn't this be the time where I focus on myself and heal and all that shit?"

Sara lifts her hand up to silence whatever Jess was about to say. "Claire, listen. I'm going to say something that's going to be hard to hear, but you need to hear it."

"Oh, shit." Jess leans back against her chair.

"You were mentally checked out of your relationship with Clay for months. You knew it was hanging on by a thread, so you did what you were supposed to do as a girlfriend, but I think deep down you knew where it was headed. You probably healed from that way before he even broke up with you. You were pissed, rightfully so, but for once you decided to give it back to someone—enter Jacks."

Damn, she might be right. I was obviously surprised that night when Clay broke up with me, but I didn't cry or anything. That came a few days later, and even then, I felt okay.

"Babe, all I'm saying is, give yourself some time to discover what you feel, and talk to him about it. He's been clear from the start, but maybe give it a few seconds to actually become something without the idea of Clay in your head." Sara smiles at me, and I roll my eyes because she's got a point.

I need to just let Jacks and I be. I need to talk to him about all this, but I'll do it when I'm ready and when things feel more developed. I don't want to jump head first into this without truly knowing how I feel. And part of me feels like I need to hit the brakes. It's too soon for me to be feeling like this. It's too soon to think about starting up a relationship with someone I barely know, and am currently fake dating. It would be too messy, and I don't want to be like Clay—moving on fast after I just went through a break up over a long relationship.

Everything I'm feeling lately has felt so big, and I need to calm down and think before making any life-changing decisions.

"Okay. That sounds good," Jess and Sara smile at me, before wrapping me in a hug. "I love you guys."

"We love you too," they mumble.

"Do you guys want to watch Jacks' game next week? It's a home game, and I'll be photographing it, but you guys can still watch."

"Ooo! Maybe we can all come back here after and drink?" Jess beams at us.

"I love that plan. Claire, ask Jacks if he's down. I have to go to class, so I'll see you guys later," Sara says as she breezes out of the apartment.

I look over at Jess. "Study date at the library?"

"I'm down. I could use some coffee."

I always feel better after I talk to my girls, but I need to learn to trust my own feelings without being scared that I'm in the wrong.

I'll trust myself again, and I already know that I can trust Jacks. I just hope he feels any semblance of emotions that I do, or this could get messy really fast, and I could find myself in the exact same position that I was when I started this whole thing.

But how do I know that it's real? How do I know that my feelings are true and not just me projecting things that I want in a relationship onto Jacks?

I'm just so damn confused.

13

Jacks

Claire and I have been having the best time over the past few weeks, and seeing her on the sidelines at my home games has me wanting this whole fake relationship thing to never end. I've never had a harder time focusing on the ice than when I look over and see Claire photographing us while wearing my jersey.

Mine.

It's the end of the second period, and Grant and I have stopped a few goals from entering. The score is 1-1, and it's been a tight game so far. We're pretty evenly matched against this team, so it could end either way. Since the period just ended, we're all headed to the locker room for a ten-minute break, but before I head in, I see my girl next to where we go in.

Fuck, she's gonna be the death of me. Claire comes over to where all the players are entering and starts snapping pictures of us. When I reach where she is, she flashes me a smile behind the camera as she continues taking pictures. I pull her away for a second. "Claire, please kiss me right now."

"Okay." And she stands on her tiptoes and presses a kiss to my mouth. *Sparks.* I'm such a goner for her. When we pull apart, she's smiling from ear to ear.

"I think I'll have the image of you in my jersey engraved in my brain for a long time, gorgeous."

"It fits me quite nicely, doesn't it?" she says as she

wraps her arms around herself.

"You look perfect, Claire. Absolutely perfect," I say as I lean down and kiss her again because I just can't help myself. "But I have to go. I'll see you after?"

"You know where I'll be."

"Always, and if I don't, you know I'll always find you." I throw a wink at her, suddenly feeling confident as fuck before I head into the locker room smiling like an idiot.

The third period ends with Grand Mountain winning, thanks to Grant and I crushing it and not letting any pucks fly by us at all. The guys and I all celebrated in the locker room, and Holt invited all of us to a party at his house off-campus to celebrate, but I have other plans. Claire invited me back to her place with a few of her friends and Justin, a nice guy that's on the team with me. I quickly shower, throw clean clothes on and am out of the locker room in the fastest time possible. I look around and see Claire standing with two other girls, still wearing my jersey.

I feel a smile form on my face before I walk over to them. Claire's back is to me, so when I get to her, I wrap my arms around her and place my head on top of hers. I know her friends know that we're "fake," but I don't care. It feels natural to do this, so I'm doing it. "Hi, gorgeous."

"Hi, Jacks." I can't see her face right now, but just from her tone of voice I can tell that she's smiling. She turns out of my hold and faces me. "You guys played a good game tonight. I got some really good shots of the team."

"I can't wait to see them," I say as I pull her arms up and place them around my neck. "Can I see the raw photos or do you want to wait until they're edited?"

Her eyebrows shoot up in surprise, before another huge smile breaks on her face. "I'll show them to you later, but I did post a few on Instagram that I took from my phone."

"I'll make sure to look at those."

"There's a few of you, so..."

"Oh, then it's my number one priority." I smile at her before I capture her mouth in another kiss. I swear ever since she kissed me in my car, I've been craving the feel of her lips against mine. I can't fucking get enough.

Someone clearing their throat breaks us both out of our weird trance we were just in. "Sorry." Claire smiles at them before turning to me and introducing us. "Jacks, this is Sara and Jess, my two best friends."

"Sara, you're her roommate, right?" I say as I reach out and offer my hand to shake.

"Yes, I am, and you're the fake boyfriend."

I stifle a laugh as Claire reaches over and smacks her on the arm. "Sara, stop."

"Claire, it's fine." I put my hand to my chest. "That's my title, and I wear it with honor every day."

"Oh wow, Claire he's a lot nicer than you told us," Jess says.

"Nice to meet you, Jess. Claire has told me how fun you guys are, and I'm excited to experience that in person tonight." I reach over and shake her hand as well, just as Justin comes over to the four of us.

"Sorry I took so long. Are you guys ready to go?" he asks us, and I'm glad to have him here. He's at least someone I'm familiar with because meeting your girlfriend's best friends is always a feat. I can tell they're psychoanalyzing me right now, and I suddenly feel on the spot. Justin brings a nice balance to the group.

"Shall we?" I ask the group while keeping my eyes steadily trained on Claire.

"We shall," she says as she grabs my hand and leads the way for us.

"No, no, no. You're wrong. Hallmark Christmas movies are wayyyy better than any Christmas rom-com that Netflix puts out," Claire yells at me as she relaxes against her couch. I accidentally let slip that I *sometimes* prefer Netflix Christmas movies over Hallmark and I realize I made a huge mistake.

This one drink that I've had is going to my head. During hockey season, I normally stay away from alcohol and shit, but tonight was cause for celebration. Not just because of our win, but because I finally met Claire's friends.

"Fine, gorgeous. You win this one. I concede," I say as I press a kiss to the side of her head.

"Jacks, did you react like a normal person when you found out that Claire likes to eat ice cream with a fork or did you act like we all did?"

"What?!" I ask him, because I feel like I heard Justin wrong. I turn to Claire. "You eat ice cream with a fork? What's wrong with you?"

"THANK YOU! It's the weirdest thing ever!" Justin says, Sara and Jess agreeing with him.

"Okay look, I've done it since I was little! My parents eat it that way too, so sue me for it! I'll never stop doing it!" Claire yells and slumps down where she sits. *God, she's adorable.*

"Okay, okay. I understand why you do it, and honestly, that's kind of adorable now that I know *why* you eat it that way."

"You guys are so cute, it's disgusting," Justin says to us.

"Well, isn't he just adorable, Claire..." Sara trails off.

I feel my girls head shift so that she's looking up at me now, and when I look over and meet her eyes, she smiles. "He is, isn't he?"

"You guys know I'm sitting here, right?" I ask them while feeling a blush spread up my cheeks.

"Yes, but we don't really care," Jess says to me as she hits my arm in a playful way.

I feel my phone start to buzz from my pocket, so I quickly excuse myself to take this call. I look down and see Holt's name light up my screen. Isn't he busy throwing a party? Why is he calling me? "Holt, what's going on?"

"Jacks, are you busy right now?" I hear his voice barely come through my phone. It's loud as fuck in his house, as usual, but I'm worried why he's calling me.

"Yeah, but whats up?"

"Can you come pick up Grant from my place? He's having a rough time, and Barnes just showed up. I don't want a fight happening, especially between two players."

"Yeah, of course. I'll be right there." I hang up, and head back to the group.

"Is everything okay?" Claire asks me.

"Yeah, I think so." I look to Justin. "Holt asked me to pick up Grant from his party. Apparently he's rough, or something."

"Grant Carter?" Jess asks.

"Yeah. He's my best friend and roommate," I tell them.

"Oh wow...I wish I knew that earlier."

"Jess, don't be gross," Claire says to her. "I'm coming with you."

"No, no. I can't ask you to do that," I say as I grab my stuff and head for the door.

"Jacks, you didn't ask, I offered. Plus, there's no way you can get him out on your own, so let's go." Claire grabs her jacket and throws it over her jersey before walking out her door. "We'll see you guys later!"

I guess she's coming with me. I say my goodbyes and apologize profusely about cutting tonight short, but Justin reassures me that we'll be doing this again in the future. By the time I get outside, Claire is a few hundred feet ahead of me and I have to jog to catch up to her. "Slow down, gorgeous. I can't keep up."

"Mhm, I'm sure you can't," she jokes. "What's wrong with Grant?"

"He's going through some shit lately, but I'm not too sure," I quietly say. I'm a shitty friend because I didn't know he was doing this bad. Is it just the whole Hads situation, or is it something deeper? Grant lost his dad a while ago and I know it's always weighed on him, but I thought he knew he could come to me for help if he needed it? Was he struggling so openly this whole time and I didn't see it? Fuck, I feel like shit.

"He'll be okay."

"I think so." The rest of the walk to Holt's place takes around ten minutes, and when we get there, the music is blaring at the same volume it was on the phone. Claire and I head into the house and I immediately spot Holt. He shoots his neck to the right, and when I follow where he told me to go, I find Grant sitting on the couch with a bottle in both of his hands. *Jesus.* He *never* drinks this much. His head lifts up, as if he knew we were walking in, and he locks eyes with me, and then they shoot next to me.

"Candy Canes! What a great surprise!" He rushes us and whisks Claire into a hug. "How is my favorite couple on campus doing?"

"We're good, Grant. How are you?" she asks him, and I see his eyes droop.

"I've been better." He looks to me. "Finally decided to join the party, did ya?"

"No. I'm here to take you home."

"Home? Why? It's a party." I suddenly find myself speechless and before I can lie to Grant, Claire speaks up.

"Because I have a surprise for you back at your place, and you can only look at it tonight." She shrugs at me, and I roll my eyes at her. Always thinking on her feet, isn't she?

"She's right, and I saw it. It's a good surprise."

Grant's eyes light up before he nods at us. "Okay, fine. Let's go then." He waves bye to everyone and makes his grand exit. I wave by to a few people, including Holt, and thankfully we don't see Ryan anywhere. Grant and him are in some weird love triangle thing with Hads. I don't know exactly what's going on, but Grant hates it. He told me that Hads has been trusting Ryan over him, and I don't blame her because Grant can come on kind of strong and dickish sometimes. I know it's fucking with his head, and I can't do a thing to help.

Some friend I am.

Claire grabs my hand and steadies my thoughts as the three of us breathe in the winter air. Grant can walk pretty well, he usually handles his alcohol better than I do, but he turns to face the two of us and starts blabbering. "Candy Canes, you look wonderful in that jersey by the way."

"Thanks, Grant. It might be my favorite thing in my closet right now."

"Random question, but do you own any pink sweaters?" Oh, here we go again.

"Claire, you don't have to answer that. Grant has declared war on both sweaters and the color pink because Hads was wearing it once."

She looks at the two of us with a confused expression on her face. "Hads as in Hadleigh Baker?"

Grant smiles at the mention of her. "Yes, that one. She's a giant pain in my ass, but that smile, and all those damn skirts she wears drive me nuts."

"She's also your tutor, Grant," I remind him.

"And?" I hear Claire say from beside me.

"Yeah, Jacks. And?"

"And nothing, isn't that a conflict of interest or something?"

"Sometimes you can't help who you fall for and when. Sometimes it just happens, and it takes your breath away." Claire says beside me as our hands swing between us. *Is she talking about Grant or herself right now?*

"EXACTLY!" Grant shouts. "Thank you, Candy Canes. Jacks of all people should know that, he's liked you ever since he saw you."

Fuck. No. He did *not* just say that did he? I definitely imagined that, right?

Wrong. I feel Claire's hand tense up in mine, and she releases our hands as we get in front of our building. I'm going to kill Grant tomorrow, and the worst part is that he might not even remember saying that. I planned on telling her that on my own time, but Grant just accelerated it for me.

As we get into the common area of our building, I turn to face her. "I have some explaining to do, but please just let me do it. I have to get Grant into bed before he does something stupid. So, I'm going to take care of him, and then I'll explain, I promise," I tell her, seeing her fiddle with the rings on her fingers. "Please be here when I come back."

She nods. "I'll be here."

I press a kiss to her forehead before dealing with Grant. When I get him to our room, I grab a bottle of water and tell him to drink it. As I'm leading him over to his bed, he looks over at me. "Do you think I'll ever be good enough for her?"

"For who?"

"Hads. I feel like I keep failing over and over again, and I don't know how to stop."

That phrase kind of punches me in the chest. I love Grant, I do, and I hate to see him hurting over something like this. He's been cheated on before and hasn't really dated in a while, so I know this is a big deal for him —putting himself out there again. "It'll be okay, Grant. You're a good guy, it might just take her a second to see that."

I don't know Hads that well, but Grant tells me how closed off she is because of stuff that happened in her past too, and deep down I feel like they're both more similar than they care to admit. I get him into bed and throw some Advil on his side table before heading back out to Claire. Fuck, I hope she's still here. I push the door open to our common area, and I don't see her for a few seconds. My heart's beating fast as I start to think that she just left without letting me explain, but a few seconds later, I find her at the vending machine we have in our common room. Every dorm has one.

I wordlessly grab my wallet out of my pocket and throw a few bucks into the machine. I press A5 and get her a bag of pretzels—her favorite kind. She's always snacking on them when I watch her edit her pictures or study. She reaches down to grab them before planting herself on one of the chairs that sits in the center of the room. Neither of us has said a word, as I take a seat across from her.

God, where the fuck do I start? What the hell am I supposed to say?

"Was what he said true?" she asks me in a low whisper.

"Yes," I say, and I see her take a big deep breath probably feeling the weight of what I just said. She knows it's been real for me the entire time. She *knows.* There's no going back now.

"So, when I approached you with my plan..." She trails off, already knowing what I'm going to say.

"Yes," I whisper back to her. "Look, I was going to tell you, I was. I thought about doing it right then and there when you asked me, but I was too much of a coward to get the words out. I thought you'd think I was insane. As I say that out loud, you probably think I'm insane right now."

"A little." She smiles.

"That's okay." I smile back at her. "Claire, you've been in my head ever since I saw you that first day and fell over on the ice. You did that by the way, your beauty practically pushed me over."

"Oh, come on, you can't blame me for that!"

"I can and I will. I've fallen over on the ice before,

but not since I was younger."

"Just keep talking, idiot." She smiles at me again, and it suddenly feels like all hope might not be lost right now. She's hearing me out, and I could jump up and down because of that.

"I knew you had a boyfriend, so I pushed it to the back of my mind—trying to pursue you and shit. I was too much of a wuss to even say a word to you at the start, so it's not like anything would've happened, anyway."

"And then I came to you with a proposition."

"Well, yeah. Freshman year went by, and every time I saw you on campus, I practically stopped breathing. All of my friends made fun of me because of how scared I was to even try to make small talk with you. But then you came to *me* with your plan, and I thought it was a sign from the universe or something. Obviously, you know what happened. I agreed to be your fake boyfriend and such, but it never felt fake to me. It always just felt like I was finally getting to know you the way I wanted to, and it felt good being with you, even knowing that you thought it was fake. I didn't care, Claire. As long as I had a small piece of you, even if it was bullshit, was enough for me."

"Oh."

"Yeah."

"It stopped feeling fake to me after that night we danced in the rain, and that scared me, so I didn't bring it up."

"Oh," I say, feeling hope bloom in my chest.

"Yeah." She sighs. "I wish you told me from the start, Jacks."

"Looking back, I wish I did too. But I can't change that. All I can do is hope that you're not too pissed at me to hear what I'm saying, Claire." Her eyes meet mine. "I like you, for real, and I don't want this to be fake anymore."

She sighs heavily and stays quiet for a few seconds. "Jacks you might be the best guy I know, but I need some time to think. It's only been a few months, and I need a minute to digest all this."

"Take all the time you need, Claire. I'll be here or not regardless of your decision." I pause before speaking again. "I'm sorry you had to find out from someone other than me, but just know that I was going to tell you. It all seemed like bad timing, and I wanted as much time with you before I probably screwed it all up."

"You didn't screw anything up. I just need to think."

I get up and sit next to her, a few beats of silence pass before I speak again. "I've never felt like this before you. I've never experienced what you make me feel, Claire."

She looks up at me, her eyes teary. "I've never felt like this either, Jacks. Not even with Clay, but it's all just a little fast."

"I understand." I press a kiss to the top of her head. "It's been an overwhelming few months. Just promise me that you'll trust what you feel. Trust that you know what's best for you, gorgeous."

She nods at me.

"I need the words, Claire."

"I promise." She looks up at me before pressing a light kiss to my cheek. "I'll see you soon, Jacks."

With that she gets up and leaves me sitting here smiling like an idiot, but feeling like the dumbest motherfucker in the world. I should've told her from the start, but something tells me that this isn't the end.

It's the beginning of something real, and I can't wait to see where it takes us.

14

Jacks

I'm sitting on my bed on this fine Thursday afternoon regretting everything I've ever done when Grant walks in. I peak over at him and he has this weird ass look on his face.

Oh God, what did he do now?

I *was* building up the courage to text Claire, but this seems like it needs my attention first. Plus, it's not like Claire would text me back. Or maybe she would.

I have no idea, but I've been giving her some space for a few days. I also yelled at Grant for spilling that tidbit of information, and when he asked why, I had to explain the whole fake dating thing to him.

Suffice it to say, it's been a weird few days. But I'm glad someone besides my parents knows now. I love going to them for advice, but I trust Grant to give it to me straight and not get my hopes up for things. I know I fucked up, and I regret not telling her about my feelings at the start, but nothing I can do will change anything now. I just have to hope that our time together—even if it was fake—was enough to at least have Claire consider something, *anything.* But this was fast. I know it was fast and so does she, and I don't want to scare her or make her second guess herself.

I *want* this. I *want* us.

But she might not, and if she chooses to go that route, I have to be okay with it. I know I'll respect any decision she makes because I'll always remember the time we spent together, even with how short it was.

Claire won't leave my mind easily, and I'm okay with that.

Grant has now encased himself underneath his sheets. He definitely fucked up, and I'm going to try my hardest not to laugh at whatever he tells me. Hads has been giving him a run for his money, and I enjoy seeing this side of Grant. It makes me feel a lot better about being a whipped fucker for Claire. I guess we're in a similar situation, and that thought makes me laugh.

I don't think Hads and Claire know how powerful they are if the two of us are *this* distraught over them. It's hilarious.

I go over to Grant's bed and yank the covers off his body. I stare at him, while waiting for him to explain what the fuck he's annoyed about.

"That was mean. I'm cold now."

"What's your deal?" I ask him, knowing that he's probably going to deflect.

"My deal? What are you talking about? My only deal right now is that I'm cold!" He tries to dramatically grab the sheets from me, probably to hide under them again, but I stretch them further away so he can't. "Rude."

"Dude, you're sulking right now."

"I am not sulking. Sulking is for sad people, and I'm not sad." *Yeah, totally. Because every time you come in here, you do this.* I'm sick of the deflection, so I rip all of his sheets clean off his bed in one swoop.

"That was for lying to me."

"DUDE! I just put those back on my bed! I'm making you put those back on." I will not be doing that.

Grant tries to reach for his sheets that I'm holding,

but I'm too quick for him. "No, not until you tell me what your deal is right now."

He sighs heavily before he finally tells me. "Hypothetically, I may have kissed Hadleigh, and she may or may not have slapped me for it."

"You did what?" *Did he just say he kissed her?* Oh, this is hilarious.

"This is all hypothetical, of course."

It's very clearly *not* a hypothetical. "So, you didn't kiss Hadleigh, and she didn't slap you?"

"Well, no, those things did happen, but the situation I'm talking about is hypothetical."

Fuck, I can't take this kid anymore. I release his sheets before I leave the room. It's funny to me how hard he's chasing after this girl but he's making all the wrong moves to do it. Then again, I haven't done much better.

"Where are you going?"

"To sign up for therapy, just hearing about your life is making me want to speak to someone."

"You're totally putting my sheets back on for me later!" he yells to me and I just shake my head at him.

But as soon as his situation melts into my mind, I feel jealous. Grant *kissed* Hads. Grant was able to kiss the girl he likes just because he wanted to.

I just hate all of this waiting, but Claire needs space. She needs to make the decision on her own terms, and if I can give her one thing, it's that.

I've never loved someone else, and I've never felt that someone I was interested in me loved me. But it felt real. Claire and I. It felt real to me the whole time, and I think it did for her too, at least toward the end. Being with her made me feel like I was whole. She made me feel like I deserved to feel how I did forever.

I've never had that before—being with someone who felt like I was coming up for air for the first time. God, this girl has fucked my head up, and I don't even care. I don't care that we're in a weird gray area right now.

I could plan some sort of rom-com worthy big gesture, but I think I'm just going to keep going on the route that I'm on. No matter how long it takes, I'm going to give her space.

In the long run, everything might work out. But for now, I'm waiting.

I'd wait forever knowing that she could eventually want to be with me.

15

Claire

I've never felt like this before you. I've never experienced what you make me feel, Claire.

I can't get anything that Jacks said to me a few days ago out of my head, and it's driving me crazy. My thoughts, my feelings, my emotions—they're all out of whack and there's nothing I can do about it.

Because it's *my* decision to make. It's my choice, and Jacks gave that to me. He's distanced himself from me the past few days and because I know him, I know that he's doing that for me. Part of my mind is screaming at me that it's too soon to jump into another relationship so quickly. The other part is reminding me that Jacks isn't like Clay. But how do I know that? How do I know that this won't turn out exactly the same? How do I know for sure? I thought Clay was the one for me, and look how that turned out, and I dated him for three whole years. Jacks and I have only been at this for a few months. How do I know *for sure* that this won't end in the exact same way as before?

"Ugh!" I try to shake off all of my thoughts, but they just won't budge. The things that he said to me that night have burrowed into my skin. *Jacks* has burrowed into my skin faster than I could've imagined, and I don't hate it.

At first, I was pissed off because he was the one so hellbent on communication, but he forgot to mention a pretty big thing to me.

But I also understand why he didn't. This whole situation—us—has been so unconventional. Hell, I was the one who propositioned him to fake date for a few months to try to get back at my horrible ex-boyfriend. *What the hell were we thinking?* Why did I think this was a good way to go about things?

Fuck. This is all too confusing, so I switch my brain to something that's like second nature to me at this point —developing my photos. I have a film camera, and right now I'm in developing some of the photos I've taken with it—in the dark room at the photography lab. This is probably my favorite spot on campus, and I often come here when I need to think or avoid my problems.

I'm doing that simultaneously right now. I'm avoiding the way I truly feel about Jacks, while trying to think of what to do next, and it's not going well. I need to just think.

We started as fake, and I even thought that too. I thought pretending with Jacks would be easy, but somewhere along the way, things got confusing and my fake feelings turned into real ones. He's just so kind and caring, and it drives me nuts.

But would it be too soon? That thought has been at the back of my mind, just lurking. Is it too soon to jump into another relationship with someone, knowing that it could end exactly like the last one did—with him falling out of love with me. How soon is too soon? A few days? Weeks? Months? How do you know you're ready to move on? How am I supposed to trust myself when I literally packed up my whole life to follow a boy I thought I loved to college, only for him to break up with me after three years? The adventure that *he* promised me when I told him I was afraid this would happen.

God, this sucks. A knock at the door of the dark room breaks me out of my thoughts, and I go to open it. Someone probably reserved the room, and they're going to kick me out. "I'll be out of your hair in a second, I'm—"

"Claire." Clay's voice stops me in my tracks, and when I look up, he's standing in front of me with a bouquet in his hand. *Oh my fucking God.* "I knew I'd find you here."

"Wh—What are you doing?"

"Can we talk?"

"I'm busy, and I have nothing to say to you." I go to close the door on him, but his foot stops it before I can. "Clay."

"Claire, please." He reaches out to touch my shoulder like he always used to, and I hate that I don't move away from his touch. "I made a mistake."

"Which one? There's been a few too many."

"I deserved that." He hands me the flowers. "These are for you, though."

I take the roses from him and immediately throw them in the garbage can. "Clay, enough. What are you doing here and what do you want?"

"I want to talk, Claire Bear." He sighs heavily, and I almost gag at the nickname he knows I hate. Oh shit, he's not trying to get back together right now, is he? "I miss you."

A few weeks ago, I would've laughed in his face at those words. But now, seeing the regret on his face makes me stop in my tracks for a second. Do I miss him? Or do I miss the idea of him that I created in my head? "Clay, I—"

He cuts me off. "Just let me explain. I thought I fell out of love for you, but being with her made me realize that you were it for me. It made me realize that I made a huge mistake treating you how I did. Seeing you with him put things into perspective."

Him. Jacks.

Suddenly I remember seeing him on the ice for the first time, and how confident he was until he looked over at me and fell on his face. It made me laugh, *he* made me laugh. Before I even knew him, he was making me smile. I remember how he stands up for me when I don't ask him too, and how the night we first kissed he let me stand up for myself in front of Clay. He *knew* I didn't need him to speak for me, and I remember laughing a lot when we were dancing in that parking lot in the rain like we were the only two people on the planet.

All Jacks has ever done is make me smile, laugh, and feel like I'm good enough to deserve those things. I remember all the butterflies erupting in my stomach after he kissed me on the cheek for the first time, and how I never, not once, felt like that with Clay. With Clay, it always felt fine. It felt right, but there was no excitement, no wanting more. I took what he gave me, even when Clay barely gave me anything.

Jacks has given me everything. The feelings, the laughs, the wanting *more*. I want to laugh with him again. I want to dance in the rain with him again. I want to be in his aura and watch him smile like an idiot, especially when he trips and falls or says some silly phrase.

Fuck. I want to be with Jacks. I know that now for sure.

What started as a plan to get back at Clay for breaking my heart has healed every broken piece of it.

No, scratch that. *I* stitched up my own heart. I'm choosing this next path. I'm choosing Jacks. "Clay, I can't do this with you. Not again."

"But—"

"I wasn't done," I sigh before continuing. "You broke my heart, Clay. I gave up my whole life for you to come here and you never even thanked me. You moved on as quickly as you fell out of love with me. I don't miss you. I don't miss what we had."

"Is that because of him? That fucking hockey player."

God, he's such a dick. "Yes. But it's also because of me. I'm not going to let you continue to play me like your own personal puppet just because you can't have me now. You want things you can't have, Clay, and now that you can't have me, you want me back."

"Claire, that's not true."

"It is from where I'm standing."

"You barely know the guy, Cee."

"Clay, stop. In the few months I've been with him, he's made me feel more than you had in three years. It's different with him than it was with you." His eyes look sad, but I find myself not caring. He dug his own grave.

"You'll regret this, and I can't wait for the day that you come crawling back to me after he breaks your heart."

"I'll see you around, Clay." I slam the door in his face and slump against it. *Damn.* That felt good. It feels good no longer having his hold on me. I've made some pretty huge decisions today, but I'm not going to jump right into them. I think I'm going to give myself a week, or however long, to affirm my decision. It feels right, but I need to learn to trust my feelings without second guessing them. I grab my phone from my bag.

Claire: Hi.

His response is almost immediate.

Jacks: Hey. Is everything okay? Are you okay?
Claire: Everything's fine. I'm just checking in.
Jacks: On me?
Claire: Yes...?
Jacks: Oh. I'm okay.
Claire: I saw Clay.
Jacks: Did he hurt you? What did he say?
Claire: Jacks, I'm fine. He would never.
Claire: He wanted to talk. He said he missed me.
Jacks: Oh. And do you? Miss him?
Claire: No. I don't, and I told him that.
Jacks: I'm proud of you.
Claire: Thanks. I'm proud of myself too.
Jacks: Good, you should be.
Claire: I still need some more time, but I promise I haven't stopped thinking about all of this. Of us.
Jacks: Take all the time you need, gorgeous. I'll be here waiting for when you're ready.
Claire: Thank you.
Jacks: Don't thank me. It's the least I could do.
Jacks: I'll see you soon.
Claire: See you soon.

16

Jacks

Two Weeks Later

It's been two weeks since I last talked to Claire and I feel like shit, but I'm choosing to remain optimistic. I'll admit when she last texted me, I was a bit nervous. She told me that she talked to Clay, and I immediately thought that she was going to say she was getting back with him, but then I remembered that wasn't what she wanted.

She just wanted to dish back some of the pain she felt to him, and it worked. But still, hearing him say that he missed her has me a bit on edge.

I just have to let it play out how it's supposed to.

I'm leaving it to the universe, or whatever.

Or maybe I'll just turn up my pre-game playlist that's filled with hype songs so I can block out all the thoughts in my head. Yeah, I like that much better. Most of the guys on the team listen to music to get pumped up before every game, including me. A lot of them listen to rap and hype music, but I prefer songs that make me feel like I'm driving fast down the road with not a care in the world.

As my playlist plays through my AirPods, I feel Grant sit down next to me and pat me on the shoulder. "You ready for our first home game in two weeks?"

I nod at him. We haven't had great luck this season on the road. Most of our wins have come from home games. "I'm ready."

"Is she gonna be here?" Grant knows everything, and even though he's been struggling with Hads, he's been here for me every day that's passed without an answer from Claire. This guy is a forever friend for sure, and I know I'll do the same for him if something goes wrong with Hads.

He's the closest thing I have to a brother, and I have Grand Mountain to thank for that.

"I'm not sure." I haven't seen her since that night Grant got drunk, so she could be skipping this game and not photographing it. I hope she didn't. I hope she's here because even if I can just catch a glimpse of her, I know it'll make me feel better.

"It'll all workout, buddy. Now, let's go kick some ass out there, okay?"

"Okay."

We're halfway into the second period, and I've been playing pretty well. Grant and I have stopped a few goals, and as I'm tracking the puck's movement across the ice, I see blonde hair in my peripheral vision.

Is she here?

I focus back on the game, and I see Grant hip check one of the opposing players. The puck wraps around the end of the rink, and I pass it down to one of my teammates to get it away from our net. The play continues, and when I look up, I see the number 86 through the glass. She's got her camera to her face, but I can see the huge smile bursting from underneath it. *She knows that I saw her.* Fuck, I'm so glad she's here.

The next thing I know, I get body checked. *Shit.*

Okay, I have to pay attention to the game or I'm going to be fucked. I reach over and grab Grant's hand as he lifts me up and we get back to the game.

As soon as the buzzer sounds to signal the end of the game, I practically rush over to the huddle so we can all leave as soon as possible. I want to talk to Claire before she leaves. I'm sure she has editing or homework to do, so I hope I can catch her.

Our coach lets us go and tells us all not to celebrate our win too hard, and I practically book it to the showers. I shake my hair out, wash my body the fastest I ever have, and as I start to change my clothes, I hear a commotion somewhere in the locker room.

"Barnes! Carter! Chill the fuck out!" Holt is *screaming* at them. I've never heard him yell so loud. I drop the shirt that I was holding, and I head to where they're at. I only see a pile of people when I get to where I assume Grant and Ryan are. I push through half of my teammates, and when I see Ryan on top of Grant about to swing at him, I grab Ryan's arm and throw him off.

"Get the fuck out, Ryan." Now *I'm* yelling, and all my teammates are staring at me. I'm not a yeller, I don't normally raise my voice at people, but Ryan being a dick—especially to Grant—needs to stop now. He immediately gets up and leaves my line of vision. I see Holt go after him, probably going to give him a talk, or at least I hope that's what he's going to do. Ryan could use it.

I reach my hand down to where Grant resides on the floor, and he takes it. I pull him up, and he doesn't say anything as he goes to his locker and grabs his shit, hurrying off to the showers. I throw my shirt on, grab my bag, and book it out of the locker room. *I hope she's still here.* Please let her be here.

I look around the rink, and a few people say hi to me and pat me on the back, telling me how good of a game we played. But all I can focus on is finding her. I'm looking all around and I don't see her. I'm about to give up hope when I see her leaning against the boards of the rink, camera in her hand, looking more beautiful than the first time I ever saw her in here.

Her eyes look up and she meets my gaze. *Fuck.* I feel like I just got punched in the chest. She smiles and motions for me to come over, so I will my feet to move over to her, and when I stop before her, I realize that I can barely feel my legs. Why am I suddenly so nervous? I run my hand through my hair a few times as I just stand next to her, absorbing as much of her space as I can.

She smiles at me again. "Hi."

Don't get your hopes up. Do not get your hopes up. "Hi, gorgeous."

"You guys played a good game. Nice win."

"Thanks." I pause, barely able to speak because of how nervous I am. Is she going to tell me her decision? Has she made it? Did I completely fuck everything up? Not knowing any of those answers is killing me right now. "So, how have you been?"

She's fiddling with her rings. It's good to know that she's as nervous as I am. "I've been okay. Doing a lot of thinking and took some time for myself. It's been nice."

"Good. I'm glad. It's what you deserved."

The two of us just stand a few inches from one another. She's leaning against the glass of the rink while still wearing my jersey, and I'm fighting the urge to pick her up, throw her over my shoulder and never put her down. I swear it's been hours before she turns and walks away from me. I find myself being disappointed because

I think this means that she made her decision, and she didn't pick me. It's fine. I knew this could happen, but—

Wait. What?

My eyes flashed to her as she was leaving, and something caught my eye. Claire's still wearing my jersey, but now, instead of my last name being on it, it says something different.

Jacks' Girlfriend. I can't stop the smile from beaming off my face, still not having moved from where I stand.

Claire turns around to look at me, a gleam in her eyes. "Do I need to wait for you to chase me or are you just going to stand there all slack jawed?" I reach her in a few strides, and before either of us can say another word, I grab her face and kiss her.

"I'll always chase you, gorgeous. Always."

Claire

"I'm holding you to that." I smile up at him when I speak. It took a week to get this jersey customized and I've been itching for this moment—him seeing me wear it. He looked so damn shocked, which makes sense, I guess. It has been a while since we've seen each other, and he probably thought my silence for two weeks meant something bad.

But now that I have him again, all feels right in the world.

But wait...do I have him?

As if he can read my thoughts, he asks me a question, "Does this mean that you made a decision?"

"I did." My voice shakes as I feel his hands come to my shoulders, as if he's steadying me. "I want us to be real,

Jacks. I don't want to be fake anymore."

He drops his head, as if in disbelief, and when he locks eyes with me again, they're starting to mist. "Fuck. Thank God. I know I said I would support you either way, but I'm glad you chose us. I'm glad you're trusting me with your heart, Claire."

"I've trusted you the whole time. You're just...the best guy, Jacks. I feel lighter when I'm with you, and I want to feel like that all the time. I thought it would be too quick, but I realized that I never felt even a fraction of this with Clay. You kind of brought me back to life, in a way. That's dramatic, but I never knew being with someone could feel like this."

"Claire, ever since I saw you, you've taken my breath away. You've barely left me head since I saw you that first day, and I can't believe how we finally got here, but shit, I wouldn't change it for the world." My eyes start to well up, but I shove that down because I don't want to cry right now. Especially not in public, where everyone can see me.

"You know you never even asked me..." I trail off, knowing that he knows what I'm talking about. My jersey might say girlfriend on the back of it, but he never asked me officially.

"Claire, do me the honor of being my girlfriend? For real this time."

"For real this time, Jacks." Just as I finish speaking, he grabs me by the waist and spins me around, as if he can't believe this is really happening. Before he sets me down, he throws me over his shoulder and walks us out of the rink. "You know I'm not going to run away from you, right? Or did you not just hear what I said to you a few seconds ago?"

"I'm not taking any chances, gorgeous. Plus, a pretty girl like you shouldn't have to walk. Especially after photographing us idiots all night."

"Fine. But I'm not fighting you on this because I like the view of your ass." It looks *good,* and I'm not gonna complain about him carrying me because I can't stop smiling. This is real. *Jacks and I are real.* I'd known this was going to be the result for a whole week, but now that it's official, I find myself wanting to scream it from the rooftops that Jacks Moore is my boyfriend. *For real.*

"Enjoy the view then. Am I taking you to your place, mine, or do you wanna go grab a bite?"

"Food sounds good right now. I forgot to grab a snack for during the game, so I'm starving."

"Damn, no granola bar? You always have one of those on standby in your bag." *It's so sweet how he knows that.*

"Did you write that on your list about me, too?"

He suddenly stops where he was walking. "How'd you know about the list?"

"I saw it when you gave me your phone in the dining hall. Your contact notes had an 'All Things Claire' section."

"And now you think I'm a creep."

I laugh as he continues walking again. "No, I thought that was the sweetest thing ever." He stills again before setting me on the pavement. "I'm serious, Jacks. You barely knew me, but you wanted to remember all the little things about me, and about my peanut allergy. It was thoughtful of you, so thanks."

He doesn't say anything, he just kisses me. And I feel the world still beneath us. This kiss feels different because it's our first official kiss as a couple. His whole body wraps me up—his scent, his wet hair falling in front of his face, his body pressed as close as he can get to mine. He slips his tongue into mine, and when he pulls back, I find myself missing the contact, so I grab his hand and we continue walking forward.

Forward as a real couple.

We may have started as fake, but nothing about the path before us will be. It's *real*, and I know the guy next to me is always going to remind me of that.

17

Jacks

Our practice ends and our coach blabs something off about playoffs being soon, but I barely hear him because my mind is on the girl I'm gonna see after this.

My girl.

Claire and I have been official for a few weeks now, and damn, it feels good showing her off around campus as mine. I can't believe I got so lucky, and I can't believe that I get to exist around her.

Grant, on the other hand, has been struggling the past few weeks, but he hasn't given up on him and Hads yet. He's in deep with that girl, and it's adorable how extra he's being about this. The other day, he asked Brendan and me to help him come up with a way to win her over, and we came up with a great idea. At least, I think it's a great idea. After a night's worth of brainstorming, he decided that he was going to annotate her favorite book for her because—according to Brendan—gifting an annotated book to someone who reads is like gold.

I stop Grant before he heads to the showers. "Have you had a chance to do what we talked about? Brendan keeps asking me, and I'm curious as well."

Grant nods at me, but looks defeated. "I've started it, but I need to get into her room to steal some things. I just don't know how to do that. Maybe I could ask one of her friends…"

"Well, it's Wednesday, and they're all at book club

right now. Maybe try asking Paige or Ella." When I say the names of the book club girls, Grant looks at me like I have three heads.

"Is that the blonde one?" he asks me and I shake my head at him. *How does he not know them by now?* The book club girls are pretty well known around this campus, but I don't think they know that. Word travels pretty easily around our small college, and most people know who you're talking about when you mention book club. Paige, Ella, Amelia, and Hads are known as the Grand Mountain book club. They're the only four members, but I keep up with them online and even on Goodreads. I enjoy reading a rom-com every now and again. Even though I prefer them in movie form, sometimes I need a good book to fall into.

Grant used to hate reading, but I think he's slowly changing his mind about that. I think he'd do pretty much anything if it helped get him into Hads' good graces. He's gone for this girl, but it's cute seeing it happen in real time.

I can't wait to tell their kids about this someday, assuming that it all works out in his favor.

I think it will, but it's probably best not to jinx it. "You're horrible at this. Just go to book club. I'm sure one of them will help you get the rest of the stuff you need." I assume he needs the right tabs, or something, because Brendan's sister also told us how important that was too. I slam my locker closed as I leave him standing where he was, and head to take the quickest shower of my life.

Ten minutes later, I'm grabbing my shit and booking it back to my dorm. I grab my phone from my pocket as I open my door.

Jacks: Are we still on for movie night?

Claire: Yes! Sara just left to go on her date, so I'm getting everything ready.
Jacks: Ooo, a date? Who is the lucky person?
Claire: Some girl she met on tinder, I think.
Jacks: Good for her. She deserves it. I hope it goes well.
Claire: I have explicit instructions to call crying if she sends me the signal.
Jacks: What's the signal?
Claire: She texts me a thumbs down.
Jacks: Ah, got it.
Jacks: I just have to change and I'll be at your place.
Claire: Sounds good!

I change out of my practice clothes and throw on some gray sweatpants and a teal shirt that I got from Hollister. I'm out the door in seconds, and I get to Claire's dorm in record time. When she opens up her door, my breath gets stolen from me yet again. I keep waiting for that to stop happening every time I set eyes on her after not seeing her for a while, but it hasn't stopped yet, and I don't know if it ever will.

Claire is just...God she's just the most beautiful person I've ever seen. I'll never get tired of looking at her. Her hand is waving in front of my face, and I need to stop zoning out in front of her all the time. She probably thinks I'm insane. "Sorry. Did you say something?"

"I said come on in," and she throws her arm out, inviting me inside again. "What were you thinking about?"

"How beautifully stunning my girlfriend is." She's wearing these red and black checkered sleep pants, with a matching button-up top.

Her cheeks flush, and I step closer to her so I can steal a kiss—only it's not stealing anymore because she's my fucking girlfriend. "What movie do you wanna watch tonight? A classic rom-com, a scary one, any of the Marvel movies...?"

The two of us walk over to her bed and sink down on the mattress as Claire loads up Netflix. She snuggles into my shoulder and pulls the blanket up so that it covers the both of us. "I think we should watch *Sleepless in Seattle*. Let's go for a classic."

She leans over and kisses me on my arm before resting her head on me again. "And just when I thought I couldn't fall more for you, Jacks Moore."

"Gorgeous, if you say my name like that one more time, I'm gonna lose my mind."

"How do I say your name?" she asks, a smile on her face. I know she knows what I'm talking about.

"Breathless," I say as I lean over and kiss her on the forehead.

"Mhm, whatever you say. Let's just watch the movie." She presses play and the movie starts. About half an hour into it, I feel Claire's hand trailing up and down my arm. And fuck, it feels good. It's like she's drawing sparks across my arm.

"I thought we were watching the movie..."

She cranes her neck to look up at me. "We are."

"Not if you keep touching me like that, gorgeous."

"But I don't wanna stop," she tells me. "I like touching you."

Fuuuuuuck. "Oh yeah? Maybe we should do something about that."

"Maybe we should."

That's all it takes for me to grab her face and kiss her. The movie continues to play in the background, but everything fades when my mouth finds hers—or anytime she's in my vicinity, to be honest. She slips her tongue into my mouth and that catches me off guard for a second, but before I can react, she moves the blanket and climbs into my lap. *Oh fuck.*

"*Claire,*" I mumble into her mouth.

She stills on my lap and I groan at the disconnection of her lips from mine. "Yes, Jacks? Is this okay?"

"It's amazing, but are you okay? You know we don't have to do this, right?" I don't want her to think we did this movie night just so it could end like this, so I want to make sure she's okay with this direction.

"I know. I want to, Jacks." Then she grinds her body while she's still on my lap, and I throw my head back because that felt fucking good. *So fucking good.*

"Fuck, gorgeous, I want you too." Our lips meet in the middle and before she can grind on my lap and drive me insane again, I flip her over so that she's on her back now. I loom over her and take her in. Her cheeks are flushed, her hair is all sprawled over the place, and she's grinding her hips into my dick, but I don't think she knows she's doing that. "Claire, if you don't stop doing that, I'm not gonna last."

"Maybe I don't want you to," she smirks.

"Are you sure about this?" I ask her and she nods. "Words, gorgeous. Use your words."

"Yes, Jacks. I want this. I want you. Please." She's out of breath already and I've barely started. *This is gonna be fun.* But I need to focus or else I'm going to embarrass myself.

"Okay, gorgeous," I say as I kiss the shit out of her lips. God, I could get drunk off the taste of her, the fullness of her lips, and the way her breathing gets heavy when I kiss her. Her cheeks flush when I pull back, and just the thought of all this is making my dick strain against my pants. *I'm fucked.* Claire told me she was nervous because it has been so long since she'd done anything of this nature. I then told her I was nervous about it because I want it to be perfect for her, perfect for us. After that conversation, we agreed to wait until it felt right. I'm excited that we both feel ready, mostly because after the intense make out sessions we keep having, I always have to calm myself down after. I never want to pressure her though, and I know we'd eventually get here. I just didn't want her to ever think that she *had* to do anything of that nature. I've told her that I'm more than okay with just having her and being in her presence.

I can't help but think that every time I see her it feels right. She feels right. It's like she's the missing disk from a movie case that I had lost and only recently found. I'll never get over how lucky I am, and I'll always try to remind her how she makes me feel—whole, complete, and like the luckiest guy on the fucking planet. "Are you sure, gorgeous?"

The smile that lights up my life appears on her face. "I trust you, baby. I'm sure."

"Can I?" I ask as I hover over her pussy.

"Yes, Jacks. Please, I'm going crazy."

"Not as crazy as I'll be after I get a taste of you." My tongue is on her seconds later, and I'm a goner. *Fucking hell.* I know for sure that Claire was made for me because I could do this all day and never get tired of it. One of her hands starts fisting my hair as she guides me exactly where she wants me, and the other is clenching her bedsheets. "Fuck, that feels good."

That's all I need to hear to continue doing what I'm doing. I focus on her clit and lightly suck on it. As

I do that, her hand grips my hair harder. "Are you close, gorgeous?"

"Yes, Jacks I—"

"Don't get all shy on me now. Come for me." She listens and shakes as I feel her coat my tongue. God, I never want this night to end. Claire has me wrapped around her finger, and I never want to unwind myself from her.

After she comes down, I notice a faint blush creep up her cheeks. "Nobody's ever done that before?"

"Gone down on you?" She shakes her head. "I'm confused."

"Nobody has ever made me come...like that." *Oh.* She's never come just from someone doing that. Fuck. I crawl up next to her as she regains control of her breathing.

"Is it bad that I'm glad that I'm the only one who has?"

That earns me another blush from her. "No. You continue to surprise me, and I can't get enough. You've ruined me for anyone else, so congratulations."

"Good. I'm yours, and you're mine, Claire. Consider me ruined too." I smile at her.

"I want to feel you. All of you."

Stars. I'm seeing stars. "Whatever you want, gorgeous. I'm all yours."

"Can I taste you?" That question catches me off guard, but she doesn't wait for my answer before pushing me back so I'm laying down on her bed, and palming my dick through my sweats.

"Fuck, that feels good."

"Do you want me to keep going?" she teases me.

"Please," I moan as she starts to pull my pants off.

Fucking hell. It's taking everything in me not to come right now. The instant my sweats are off, her mouth is on my dick. *Oh my God.* She takes me in her mouth and just the feel of her sucking me off is sending me over the edge, but then she wraps her hand around my shaft and pumps me while her mouth still works me.

If heaven exists, it's here with her right now.

"Claire, fuck, please don't stop." She groans around my cock while she continues to jerk me off. When she takes her hand off a few seconds later, I groan at the loss of contact, but then she takes her tongue and drags it up my entire dick before taking me fully to the back of her throat. "*Fuck.*"

As she relaxes her throat and allows all of me in, I can feel myself start to come apart. "Not yet, baby. I know you can last longer."

I really can't. "Claire, don't play this game with me right now." With that, her mouth is back and I feel my dick reach the back of her throat again, but this time she cups my balls too. "Baby, I'm gonna come down that pretty little throat if you don't stop driving me crazy."

She looks up at me, and the sight of her eyes locking on mine while she takes my dick in her mouth is one I'm memorizing for later because *fuck*, she looks perfect. "Do it, Jacks."

She doesn't have to tell me twice and I come. *Hard.* The hardest I've ever come before, even just using my hand, and fuck it feels damn good. "*Claire, Jesus, fuck.*"

When the haze of my orgasm subsides and we get all of our clothes back on, I kiss her. "What was that for?"

"What I can't kiss you because I want to?"

"No, you can, I didn't expect you to kiss me after I —"

"Claire, please don't finish that sentence because if you tell me that Clay never liked to do that, then he's a fucking dumbass. That's not how I do things, okay? That's not how *we* do things."

She smiles at that, which causes me to smile back at her too. "Okay, noted."

I lean in and kiss her again, swiping my tongue into her mouth, and when we pull apart, we're panting again—as if we didn't just do what we did for the past half an hour. "Movie time?"

"Yeah, but we might have to rewind it..." She trails off with a laugh and I join her as we get comfortable on her bed again. I notice that ten minutes into our rewatch, she's dozed off on my shoulder, so I cover us with the blanket and stay still for the rest of the night so that she doesn't wake up.

This was one of the best nights ever, with the best girl ever, and I wouldn't have it any other way.

18

Claire

"Guys, I can't wear a strapless, three sizes too small dress to this banquet! That's like the worst idea I've ever heard!"

"Why not? It's hot," Sara tells me.

Jess laughs her ass off as she continues to look through my closet. Jacks invited me to his year-end hockey banquet as his plus one, but he forgot to tell me until the last minute.

The banquet is tonight and I have nothing to wear. *Nothing.* But I can't be too mad at my boyfriend, I'm just glad he asked me to go with him.

Clay never asked to go to any baseball stuff with him, but Jacks has changed that for me. Over the past few months, Jacks has slowly changed everything for me. He's shown me what a relationship *should* be, and I've never once questioned his loyalty for me. He comes over and does movie night with me and the girls. I watch his games while photographing them and after we go out with the team and they all make fun of us but when Jacks leaves the table, they tell me how happy they are for us. It's been the best few months with him, and I can't believe I almost missed out on it. I can't believe I almost let my fear get in the way of this.

A few weeks ago, I told my parents about Clay and how everything blew up. They were supportive as I word vomited the story to them over a two-hour phone call.

They even offered to drive down for a few days to take my mind off things, but I told them I was fine.

And then Jacks came over and I spent an hour explaining *that* to them. They were worried at first, of course, but when I told them about Jacks and I, I knew they saw the look on my face and the twinkle in my eye.

This one is a good one, and Jacks even sat through their badgering of questions over the phone for an hour—with a smile on his face the entire time.

Clay barely interacted with my parents unless he had to. By the end of the phone call, Jacks had my dad's phone number and a promise to teach him how to fish when he comes to visit Delaware.

I was *shocked*, but glad that he had made a good impression because my dad can be...tough. All of my friends in high school were scared of him—some of them still are, and I still laugh as I tell my dad about that.

"What about this one?" Jess asks me as she pulls a pink dress out of my closet that I've never seen before.

"What the hell is that?" I wonder as I walk over to her. I look at the dress—it's a satin dress with a tiny slit at the bottom. It goes to around my knees, and when I try it on, it fits perfectly. *Where did I get this?*

"Wait hold on, something fell off it." Jess then reaches into the back of my closet and pulls out a small note. She reads it, blushes, and then hands it over to me.

I know I asked you to be my date at the last minute,
but I'm hoping this dress makes up for it.
It's beautiful, but not as beautiful as the
girl who will be wearing it.
Thank you for being you.

−J

I can't stop the smile that creeps over my face as I put the note down. *Why is he so perfect?*

"Oh my God, and I thought he couldn't get swoonier..." Sara says as she reads the note.

"I need to buy a casket. Seeing all this adorable and happy shit from you two is going to kill me." Jess sits down, but she smiles as she does, so I know she's kidding, if only partially.

"I don't even know what to say right now." I pause as I fluff my hair out a bit. "He's the best, I—" I have to stop the emotions from creeping up my throat or else my makeup that I spent way too long doing will be ruined.

A knock at my door stops the happy tears from falling, and Sara goes to answer it while I put my shoes on —white heels with cute straps. They go with everything, and they'll give me a bit of height with Jacks, so it's a win-win. "Well don't you gentleman look devilishly handsome tonight."

"Hi, Sara," Jacks leans over to hug her and she returns it. It brings a smile to my face at how much he loves getting to know my friends. He cares about me and my life, and the people I choose to have in it, and I wish I could explain how much that means to me. Words just don't cut it.

"This is my friend, Grant. Grant this is Sara and Jess." Jacks formally introduces Grant to my friends. They've met in passing, but never officially.

"Hi. Nice to meet you guys." He smiles, but I can tell he's hurting on the inside. Jacks told me that tonight was going to be rough for him, and that we should do our best to keep his spirits up. I know all about the whole Grant, Ryan and Hads situation, and I *hate* Ryan, so I'm always firmly on Team Grant. But unfortunately, Hads is going to the banquet with Ryan and not him.

It kills me to see Grant like this. He's normally so full of life, but lately he just looks defeated, and I hate that. Hads will come around, though. I don't know her that well, but I know she's a smart girl.

Jacks takes one look at me and clutches his hand to his chest. I slowly walk over to where he stands in my doorway and look up at him. Before I can speak, he kisses me.

When he pulls away from me, he eyes my body in the dress that he bought me. "You look absolutely stunning tonight."

"I had a wonderful stylist," I chuckle at him.

"Don't keep our girl out too late, boys! We're not afraid of hunting you down if Claire comes back late!" Jess yells to us as I quickly grab my purse and close the door.

The drive to the banquet hall is short and quiet. Nobody said a word as Jacks drove us here. Now we're sitting our table, and Jacks is patting Grant on his back, silently letting him know that he's not alone. That he's here with him.

I love how close they are. It's easy for anyone to tell that they really care about each other. I know a lot of people talk about how sports teams often become a family, but these two really are brothers. Just seeing their interactions up close have showed me that. They would go to war for one another, and it makes me smile knowing that Jacks has someone like that in his life. I know Grant would do anything for Jacks, and vice versa.

Grant hasn't taken his eyes off the door since

we got here. Granted, we were early, but I don't want him obsessing about seeing Ryan and Hads together. I'm worried about him, so I try to make some conversation. "How are you doing, Grant?"

"I'm alright. I just want to get tonight over with." *Understandable.*

"Well, if you want someone to dance with for a song or two, I'll dance with you unless Jacks steals me first. I don't want to see you sulking all night. You deserve to have fun after the season you had." I pat his hand because even if the team didn't end up having the greatest finish to the season, Grant did amazing. He's even getting the award tonight for top defensive player for the team this year. He had the most time on the ice and the most turnovers this season. Jacks also had the most blocks this season, so he'll be getting an award tonight too. I'm so damn proud of these two. They make a hell of a team out on the ice together.

"Thanks, Claire, I appreciate it." Then his gaze turns blank, and when I follow it to the door, I notice Hads is walking in with Ryan on her arm, but her eyes are on Grant. *Oh my God.* I can *feel* the tension from here. So many unspoken words pass through them at this moment, and I wish I could snap them both out of it and lock them in a room so they can talk it out.

But Jacks told me not to meddle, and to let it take its course, so I'll pretend like I haven't seen or felt anything between those two.

Except when Ryan flashes a middle finger at Grant that he thinks nobody sees, it takes all of my willpower not to throw one back because I know Grant won't. He's too good of a guy for shit like that.

Grant excuses himself, and I don't stop Jacks when

he follows him to the bathroom. *Fuck.* It's killing me not being able to help. Hads walks by our table, and I stop her to say hi. "Hads, I love your dress! It looks amazing on you."

She smiles at me, but I can tell it's a fake one. Something's bothering her, but I doubt she'd tell me. "Thanks, Claire. Tell Jacks that I say hi."

"I will."

"You two are adorable together, by the way. I saw that picture on your Instagram of you guys a few months ago. It was really cute." She fiddles with her dress, as if she's uncomfortable in it all of the sudden, so I do my best to ease her nerves.

"Thanks. I saw that you also like photography. Maybe we could get together and shoot some pictures sometime?" I may have stalked her Instagram after Jacks updated me on everything going on.

To that, she smiles widely at me. "I'd like that."

"Great. Just email me and we'll get something set up!"

"Sounds good," she looks around nervously. "I better get to my table."

"Have fun tonight, Hads."

"I'll try," she says as she walks over to sit next to Ryan. Huh, I guess it's a good thing that Ryan isn't sitting at our table. I guess their coach decided to divide the sophomores into two tables since there are so many of them.

The boys come back a few moments later just as dinner starts. The buffet and short awards ceremony go off without a hitch, and before I know it, Jacks and I are slow dancing to a song with Ryan and Hads not far from us. I see Grant watching them from over Jacks' shoulder, and for the twentieth time tonight, my heart sinks through my chest.

"Come back to me, gorgeous." I feel a hand on my face as I look up at my boyfriend's beautiful eyes. "Where did you go just now?"

"Sorry. I just…I feel bad that we're having so much fun while Grant looks like a sad puppy. Are you sure there's nothing we can do to help?"

"It'll work out in the end. We just have to trust that it will. I don't know how long it'll take, but I have faith that everything will be okay."

I lean my head into his chest as we sway to the music. "Okay."

"Just enjoy this moment with me, please. I'm having the best time with you here on this dance floor."

I listen to my wonderful boyfriend and when the song ends, I go over to the table and offer a dance to Grant. He accepts but as the next song plays—*Can I Be Him* by James Arthur—he tenses up. "We can wait for another song, Grant. I'm going to grab water. Do you want one?"

"Uh, sure. That sounds good."

I turn to Jacks. "Babe, do you want one?"

"I'll take whatever you want to get me." *Swoon.* I head to the drink station and run into my friend Justin at the table.

"Hey, girl. You look stunning, tonight. How's everything?"

I smile at him as I grab three waters from the cooler. "Everything is surprisingly amazing, especially after the shitty start I had to this year."

"I'm happy for you. You deserve all the happiness that Jacks can give you. Just let me know if he pulls some Clay shit. I don't think he would, he's too good of a guy, but still. I'm here for you always. Never forget that."

"I won't, Justin. Thank you. Give my love to Miles, okay?"

"I will if I can ever get him off the dance floor! See you later!" Justin walks back to his guy and joins him in a slow dance, and my heart melts. *They're just too cute.* As I walk back to our table, I see Grant booking it out of the venue toward the parking lot. *What?* When I reach our table, I see Jacks looking confused as I am.

"What's going on?" I ask him as I set our waters down.

He shakes his head. "I'm not too sure."

"Do you wanna dance?"

"Only with you." He pulls me onto the dance floor and I have vivid memories of us dancing in the rain together. It hit me before that maybe it wasn't all fake in the beginning, and that maybe I just felt that way because of how scared I was that it could start to become real— Jacks and I. But now, I'm wholly content with what we are. He's my boyfriend, for real, and I'm his girlfriend, for real.

It feels good to be with him. It feels good knowing that I'm his and he's mine.

Around five songs later, Jacks pauses our dance and practically runs off the dance floor, and I follow him. Grant's hustling back in here, with no jacket on, and his eyes are locked on someone across the room. It's like he's not even in his body right now, and that scares me. *What the hell is going on?*

"Jacks, let me go." Grant is *seething*. I've never heard him angry before.

Jacks shakes his head as he drags Grant out of the banquet hall we're in. "What happened out there?"

"J, I need to do something. I *need* to punch the shit out of him."

"You know that won't solve anything," Jacks reminds him before he says something to me. "Gorgeous, can you take my keys and bring the car around?"

I'm about to answer when Grant speaks first. "No, we're not leaving until I find out what that son of a bitch did to Hads."

"What?" I whisper. "Did Ryan—"

He cuts me off. "Yes, he did. And when I find out exactly what he did to make her step away from me when I tried to comfort her, I'm going to make him *hurt*."

"Gorgeous, go get my keys from the table and pull the car around." Jacks tells me again, his hands still pressed firmly against Grant's chest to stop him from moving.

"Okay, I will." I don't say anything else as I do as I'm told. When the boys get into the car a few minutes later, I say nothing as I notice the dry tears on Grant's face before I peel out of the parking lot and head toward Grand Mountain.

19

Jacks

Two Weeks Later

"You look like shit," I say to Grant as I hop onto his bed that he's currently laying in.

"What happened to being nice to me while I'm down?"

"Downtime is over. Take a fucking shower, Grant." He hasn't been taking the best care of himself lately, and I was going easy on him at first, but I can practically see the cartoon smell lines coming off him. He needs a long shower, and maybe some Taylor Swift music to get him in better spirits.

"Hey, fuck you. At least you have someone to take a shower for. I'm sitting here dying a slow death, most likely. The longer it takes her to decide, the worse it's looking for me."

"You don't know that. Don't jump to conclusions," I say as I throw his towel at him.

"Well, what the fuck do I do? What do I do if she realizes I will never be enough for her? What if she gets bored with me in the future? The what-ifs are running through my head and won't stop!" He's pacing now, and I'm sitting at my desk just letting him get all of this out. It reminds me of the beginning of the year when the thing he was worried about was his failing grade. *How did we get here?*

"Where do I go, Jacks? I feel lost without her. I

feel *so* lost. I feel like a kite with no strings attached, just floating freely into the atmosphere. The only thing running through my mind has been her since I walked away from her on those goddamn steps the other day! I just—I don't—" I cut off his ramblings with a hug because he looked like he could use one. I feel his body shake a little, and when we pull back, I notice a few tears have fallen.

Damn, he's fucked in the head about this...I guess I can't blame him, especially since he doesn't know what the hell happened that night. If this was Claire, it would've driven me crazy by now.

"What if she never realizes how she feels? What should I do? Am I supposed to let her move on to someone else while I watch from a distance? Jacks, what do I do? Please tell me what to do."

"I can't. You have to hope that this works out. I think it will. I've told you many times that how she looks at you isn't how you look at a friend. She needs time, and that's okay. Whatever happened with Ryan had to have shaken her a lot for this to affect her so much."

"I told you not to say his name around me." He glares at me, and I suddenly feel like shit again.

"I know. I'm sorry. I'm just saying that we don't know what happened in that hallway."

"We could maybe find out, couldn't we?"

"Oh, I really don't like that face you're making right now. What's going on in your head?"

"We could confront him. Make him tell us what happened. A douche like Ry—like him would want to rub it in, and I don't know, be a dick about it like everything else."

"What should we do then?" I ask him.

"Do you know where he is?"

"It's Saturday. He's probably at the gym or something."

"Let's go find him then."

"Alright, let's go." He grabs his keys before stopping at the door, not fully wanting to leave yet. "Okay, maybe I should shower first."

"Yeah, that's a good idea." I sit at my desk as I wait for Grant to shower and put some fresh clothes on. I grab my phone and call Claire while I wait. She picks up on the second ring.

"Hi, babe! Are you headed over now?"

"There's been a sudden change of plans. Grant and I have to do something before I come over for movie night. I'm sorry, gorgeous."

"It's okay. Tom Hanks and Meg Ryan will still be here no matter when you come over. Is Grant okay?" God, I love how kind she is.

Oh.

Love.

I'm in love. I'm *in love* with Claire. The revelation stops me in my tracks. I thought the first time I admitted to being in love with someone would feel revolutionary in a way.

But it only feels right. My body warms as I come to the realization.

I love Claire. I love my girlfriend more than anyone on this planet.

"Jacks, hello? Did I lose you?"

Her voice breaks me from my thoughts, and I smile. "No, gorgeous. I'm still here, sorry. Grant is finally showering, but we just have a small thing to do before I see you."

"You're not going to tell me what you two are doing are you?"

"Of course, I am. We're going to find Ryan and get him to tell us what the fuck he did to Hads."

"Oh. Is that the best course of action? Isn't Grant still extremely pissed off?" *She makes a good point...*

"It'll be fine, I promise. I'll reel Grant in if he gets to be too much."

"Good. Be careful. I've never liked Ryan, but I don't want you guys to suffer if you do something stupid."

"We'll be careful," I say as Grant comes back in and throws his clothes on. "I have to go. I'll see you later?"

"Sounds perfect."

Say it. Tell her you love her. "Bye." *Coward.*

"Bye!"

"Are you ready?" Grant asks me, and I nod as we head out of the door to go look for Ryan.

As Grant and I walk out of the gym after an enlightening conversation with Ryan, I shake my hand off. *Punching someone hurts like a bitch.*

But the asshole fucking deserved it.

Ryan launched into this whole ridiculous spiel about how Hads strung him along for months and was "asking for it." So, before Grant could hit him, I did. And now my knuckles hurt, but I couldn't stop thinking about the fact that he could've been talking about Claire, and that *really* pissed me off.

Plus, I used his logic back at him. I technically didn't knock him out if he was asking for it, which he was, based on all the foul-mouthed shit he was saying. God, he's such a prick. It blows my mind that some people think the way that they do.

Grant heads off to get some ice for my hand, but I suddenly only care about seeing one person right now. I book it out of the gym, send a text to him that I'm headed to Claire's, and I reach her door in a few minutes. I knock with my left hand because my right is still bleeding from the impact of hitting Ryan's jaw, and when she opens the door, her eyes immediately go to my hand resting at my side.

"Jacks Moore, I thought I told you to be careful!" I don't have time to answer before she pulls me into her room, and sits me down on her desk chair. "Did Ryan do this? I swear to—"

"Uhhhh, I did, technically..." I trail off as I look up at her. *God, she's perfect.*

"What happened, baby?" she asks me as she grabs a first aid kit from her desk drawer.

"Ryan was speaking, so I shut him up."

"What did you do?"

"I punched him in the face before Grant could. I didn't want Grant to regret it, plus it might hurt his chances with Hads if she finds out that he hit Ryan, even if he did deserve it." She takes some small ice packs and tapes them to my hands so the swelling can go down. She's just mindlessly doing all of this as I tell her what Ryan said to Grant and I. She looks shocked, but not that surprised because she voices how she and her friends never really liked him either.

"Jacks, come rest. It'll help take your mind off the pain. Do you want some painkillers? I think I have some around here somewh—"

"I love you." *Oh my fuck, did I just blurt that out?*

She stills where she stands and slowly turns

around to face me as my legs dangle off her bed. "What?"

"Fuck, I've never done this before, and I've already fucked up." I pause, gathering the words that I want to say to her, but nothing comes to mind, so I just speak. "I love you, Claire Canes."

"But you've never been in love before..."

"I know, but I love you. I think all this time I was saving those three words, those seven letters, for you. I think I knew deep down that I was only meant to say them to you, Claire." Fuck, I feel like I'm gonna cry in a second. Nothing I ever say will ever tell her how much I truly mean it, but I'll spend as long as she'll give me trying to prove to her that she deserves all my love.

"Jacks, I—"

I cut her off because I don't want her to feel pressured or anything. "Baby, you don't have to say anything—"

Then she cuts me off. "I love you, Jacks Moore. I think I've loved you since that day we danced in the parking lot in the pouring rain. *God,* I love you. So much. Thank you for redefining that phrase for me."

"Redefining? What do you mean?" I ask her, suddenly nervous.

"With Clay, I thought love was supposed to be quiet and simple, with none of the longing for more. I was always content with him, and there was no excitement anymore, but I was prepared to spend the rest of my life like that. I thought I was destined for a life of subpar love that didn't make me feel...anything. But with you, God, with you it's explosive. Every time I see you, you take my breath away because of how lucky I feel to be with you— to be in your presence. I know for a fact that I would go through all the shit I did with Clay, just to know that I had a chance with you after."

Fuck, I'm crying right now, and I wipe a few tears from her cheeks where she stands between my legs, her face inches from mine. "Claire, I'd wait forever and ever for you if I knew you'd be the first girl I'd ever love."

"Was I worth the wait?" she asks through tears.

"Of course, you were, baby."

"I think you put my heart back together, so thank you for loving me how you do, Jacks. Thank you for loving me despite how much of a mess I was when we met."

My heart is practically bursting out of my chest right now. "Claire, for worse or for better, I love you either way. I fucking love you, and I'm not fucking going anywhere. I want to love you as long as you'll have me."

"How about forever and ever?" She smiles, repeating my words from a few seconds ago.

"That sounds good to me, gorgeous." And then I lean in and kiss her until we're breathless, and the two of us are repeating how much we love each other as if we'll stop breathing before we can say it again.

I got my girl.

20

Claire

August 2022

Hads: We're meeting at the library, right?
Claire: I think so?
Hads: Even if we didn't agree on it, the boys will follow us wherever anyway, so I say we keep it with the library.
Claire: Good point, and that sounds good!
Grant: You guys realize we're in this chat too, right?
Jacks: Yeah...
Jacks: Also, I don't think we're that whipped.
Grant: Oh please. I saw the photos Claire posted on Instagram the other day. How was it getting all that whipped cream out of your hair?
Hads: Whipped cream?
Claire: It was for a photoshoot! And the pictures came out great!
Jacks: Grant, you're the one already planning your couples Halloween costume and Hads is literally going to walk you like her dog, so I don't wanna hear it.

"That was mean," I say to Jacks as we walk toward the library together.

"He started it! He's the king of being whipped for Hads, or did you forget all the stuff he said last semester while he was chasing after her?"

I haven't forgotten, but did my boyfriend forget that I have him wrapped around my finger too?

Jacks and I have been going strong since last semester, and I wouldn't have it any other way. Along with Hads and Grant finally figuring things out, the four of us often have study dates, hangouts, and double dates together. It's been amazing, and I've found comfort in these three people around me.

Hads and I clicked almost instantly. We stayed in touch over the summer and when we got back to campus last week, we've met up a few times for some impromptu photoshoots and coffee trips. It's fun being friends with someone where you're both dating two best friends. It's a different kind of relationship, and I'm forever grateful that Hads figured out her feelings for Grant. It's absolutely adorable to see them together.

Jacks and I are about to head into the library when someone runs into my shoulder, and I drop a few of my things. "I'm so sorry, I must not have been paying attention—" I stop my words because I don't expect to see the person who's standing in front of me right now.

"No, Claire. I'm the one who should be apologizing."

Evangeline Hopkins—the girl that Clay cheated on me with—is staring back at me, dumbfounded. I heard that she and Clay broke up, or split up, or whatever, a few weeks ago. Then I also saw Clay getting real cozy with another girl at the dining hall the other day, so I guess some people can't change.

I feel a calm energy wash over me as Jacks hands me back all the stuff I dropped on the sidewalk. So, I grab her hand and say the words that have weighed on my chest ever since I met her last year. "No apology is necessary. It wasn't your fault."

I think she knows that I'm not talking about her running into me. I can tell because she squeezes my hand a few times before walking away. I turn to Jacks and smile at him, feeling more weightless than before. "Is everything okay? I expected that to be more awkward or tense."

"Yes, my love. Everything is perfect. I never really blamed her for how things went down, and it was time that she knew that."

"I love you, you know. I love how kind you are." Jacks throws his arm around my shoulder as we sit down at our usual library table and wait for Hads and Grant.

"I love you too, Jacks. I love how sweet you are." He taps a finger on my nose and I feel my lips upturn into a smile unconsciously. He makes it easy—loving him, and being loved by him. I lean over to kiss him before I hear someone groan near us.

"Oh, come on, Candy Canes. I've seen you guys kiss enough while you over at the apartment, but now I have to see it in public?" Grant complains as he sits down in our booth.

"Pretty boy, will you just let them be happy? God knows they deserve it." Hads flashes me a wink in solidarity as she sits down across from me.

"Thank you, Hads. Grant, last time I checked, you were the one who threw Hads over your shoulder on the way to class the other day...in broad daylight!" I make fun of him because I know he doesn't care about PDA. He likes pushing our buttons.

"Grant, you were the one who wanted to get us all matching shirts, so I don't wanna hear it." Jacks references the twenty-five long slideshow presentation that Grant made and showed us the other night. It was about the benefits of having matching shirts correlated to the longevity of being a couple. It was *hilarious* how much effort he put into it, and we all eventually conceded and agreed to get them.

Grant ordered them instantly, and they should be here next week.

"How's the first week been for you guys? Is junior year giving you hell yet?" I ask the two of them.

"It's been pretty chill for Jacks and I. At least I'm not failing yet like I was at this point last semester." Grant then holds his hand up, to which Jacks gives him a high five. *Idiots.*

"You guys are ridiculous." Hads rolls her eyes at them.

"Grant, I think you'd be thankful for that failing grade since it led to your girl over here," I tell him.

"I am! I'm just saying that this semester is off to a way better start, and I'm grateful for that."

"Me too," Jacks says, and I have to fight the urge to kiss him again. The four of us then continue talking over coffee for a few hours as other students trickle around us in and out of the library.

Last semester may have been one of the weirdest times of my life. But I'd do it all over again to get to this point.

Jacks redefined the meaning of the word love for me. I've never had someone do that for me before— redefine what a word means to me, but he did.

He's showed me that it's not about the words or the shit that people say to you. It's about the actions that they take to *show* you how much they mean to you. Jacks does that for me every day, whether it's modeling for my pictures, helping me pick between which edits I like better on my pictures, or watching all of my favorite movies with me. He always shows me that he's here, and in it for the long haul.

And when we go back to his apartment tonight, I know for certain that he'll mouth the words of whatever movie we watch together. He's memorized most of my favorites, and I'll never get tired of seeing him next to me while we watch them.

There's one thing I know for certain, though. The way he loves me is better than any movie I've ever seen.

He puts them to shame, and I wouldn't want my life to be any other way.

THE END.

ACKNOWLEDGMENTS

As always, I need to think the people who I couldn't do this without. Lexi and Hannah, thank you for being along on this ride with me. I also commend you guys for putting up with my insanity—like when I wrote this whole thing and didn't tell you guys until I was done. Oops! Hannah, as always, you design the most beautiful covers ever, and I feel so lucky to know you. Lexi, who's practically my everything when it comes to these books, I am so lucky to have a friend like you. Both of you always put your all into this little adventure that started out as a hypothetical, and I don't think I'll ever have the proper words to say thank you. I love you both so much. Grand Mountain forever.

Fabian, thank you for allowing me to use that phrase that you and Kyle often used to annoy me. I guess it came in handy after all!

Bri, first of all, you're a legend for coming up with part of this title. I guess creative genius runs in your family, and thank you times a million for everything that you do—including deal with Lexi and I's insanity.

My beta readers—Sof, Laur, Drew, Amy, and Meaghen. I love you guys! Thank you for your hard work into making my stories shine much brighter, and make a thousand times for sense than they did originally.

Drew, thank you for helping me with all the biology language. I appreciate your input so much, and even the worksheet that you sent me so I could properly explain it. I'm glad your suffering over bio could be translated into something for this book. A win is a win, right?

To Lauren, Ella, Jordy, Kat, Maine, Liv, Tejas, and anyone else who fell in love with Jacks when he was first introduced in book one, this novella is for you. Thank you for keeping the delusions in my brain alive because it helped me come up with this idea one night when I was in my room listening to Fearless.

To you, the reader. Thank you for taking a chance on my little universe. I truly couldn't do this without you! Thank you for reading my words and taking a chance on me! I love you all times a million!

ABOUT THE AUTHOR

Emily Tudor creates characters and stories about platonic and romantic love for anyone and everyone. She lives in the state of New York and loves listening to music and creating stories. She loves Marvel movies, the song *mirrorball* by Taylor Swift, and buying too many books when she already has many to be read at home.

You can find her on Instagram at:
@authoremilytudor
@emil.yslibrary

Printed in Great Britain
by Amazon

35125047R00097